F
BRI

Bridgers, Sue Ellen

Keeping Christina

2376

$14.89

DATE			

BAKER & TAYLOR

KEEPING CHRISTINA

SUE ELLEN BRIDGERS

KEEPING
CHRISTINA

HATHAWAY HIGH

HarperCollins*Publishers*

Library of Congress Cataloging-in-Publication Data
Bridgers, Sue Ellen.
    Keeping Christina / Sue Ellen Bridgers.
        p.   cm.
    Summary: When she befriends Christina, the new girl in school, Annie does not suspect that there is
more to her than meets the eye and that Christina will have a huge impact on Annie's family and her
oldest friends.
    ISBN 0-06-021504-6. — ISBN 0-06-021505-4 (lib. bdg.)
    [1. Friendship—Fiction.   2. Schools—Fiction.   3. Honesty—Fiction.]   I. Title.
PZ7.B7615Ke   1993   92-22061
[Fic]—dc20   CIP
                                                                                  AC

For Pat Ross

1

Our plan was to meet in the band room before the first bell and I was in a hurry. My book bag swung off my shoulder as I pushed through the heavy door and, angling to catch it, I didn't even see the girl in front of me until I had plowed into her with a solid thud.

"Sorry," I said, stumbling backward to right myself. I was already trying to scan the bulletin board across the room for the bright-yellow paper of the cast list.

"It's okay," the girl said, but several composition books were scattered and she went to her knees to retrieve them.

Kneeling to catch a rolling pencil, I couldn't help but notice a patch of frayed yarn on the under-side of her sweater sleeve. "Here." I held out the pencil. "I'm Annie Gerhardt." The girl still hadn't looked at me. "And you're——"

"Christina Moore."

"Oh, I remember now," I said, getting up. "You're in my English class."

When Christina stood beside me, I saw she was slender, almost willowy. She probably auditioned as a dancer, I thought, looking at her straight on because suddenly there was no avoiding those blue eyes full of deep stares. She had the most perfect skin I've ever seen and an eager mouth that seemed to be quivering between a smile and a grimace.

How could I have missed somebody with these looks? I wondered, because even without makeup she had an exotic face framed in thick tangly curls.

"Didn't you write a poem Ms. Langley read to us?"

Christina nodded, and her eyes disappeared under a fringe of dark hair. "I sit at the back on the same aisle as you."

"Well, the poem was great. You ought to be in front of all us dummies."

"I came here after Thanksgiving, so all the good seats were taken." Her voice was small and weary, like she was used to describing disappointments.

"Oh, yeah. Well." Before I could think of something sympathetic to say, Jill came through the door, a patchwork of colors in her jacket and bright hat. Her nose and cheeks were dark with a skier's tan.

"You're back!" I screamed and we fell toward each other, hugging and laughing. "How was Steamboat? Tell me everything! The guys! Gosh, I know they were gorgeous. No, don't tell me! I don't want to know."

"It was great," Jill said. "Lots of good powder. A Jacuzzi in the room. Gigantic fireplace in the lodge." Arm in arm, we moved toward the bulletin board. "And you, what did you do?"

"The same old boring stuff. I ended up going to the Pickenses' New Year's Eve party with Mom and Dad—and Greg, of course—you wouldn't believe the big point Amanda made of inviting him. I think she called every hour on the hour the entire day. And the dress she had on! A black slinky thing with beads dripping off it. It had to be vintage."

"Amanda can get away with clothes like that," Jill said. "Me, I'd look ridiculous. Well, here it is!" The cast call for *Kiss Me, Kate* was handwritten in Ms. Dalton's bold print. "Amanda Pickens— Lilli/Katharine," she read. "Peter Hughes— Fred/Petruchio."

"Just what I expected," I said. "After all, Amanda's got a terrific voice and Peter's the best actor in school."

"According to you." Jill ran her finger down the list. "Dan Coleman got Bill/Lucentio!"

"Now who's impressed?" I teased.

"He's such a smart aleck!" She was trying to abort one of her giggling fits.

"And you think he's so cute."

Jill was ignoring me. "I'm the maid!" She frowned, then brightened again. "Well, at least I don't have to play two parts. Who wants to have to practice all the time, anyway? 'Another op'ning, another show,'" she sang, swaying, palms lifted, fingers splayed as if she intended to tap dance. "Wait a minute, who's this? Christina Moore got the part of Lois/Bianca. Who in the world is that?"

"Sh-h-h-h, that's her," I whispered. "Hey, Christina, congratulations. You got Lois!"

"I was afraid to look," Christina said, coming forward.

"Christina's in our English class," I said. "Remember, she wrote that poem about being dead."

"You wrote that?" Jill asked. "It gave me the creeps. It was good though."

4

Christina was peering over our shoulders to see the list.

"Well, let her look," I said, and we parted to let Christina in.

❧

That afternoon during last period, the cast of the winter musical gathered in the band room to hear Ms. Dalton, the drama coach, and Mr. Dorsey, the music director, explain the schedule. I was there, too, because as usual I was first-chair clarinet.

"Just one of the grunts," I always said, knowing someone would invariably counter with "But you're the concertmaster. That's as important as anyone in the entire show."

Which, of course, it was. Mr. Dorsey depended on me because he was having to bring in violins from the community—a twelve-year-old virtuoso and two retired music teachers who had studied violin in college and played only when coerced. The rest of the orchestra was comprised of band students who performed with varying degrees of skill and enthusiasm. To get them there at all, Mr. Dorsey had to threaten them with low grades in instrumental class.

"Rehearsals start next Monday," Ms. Dalton was saying. She was thick bodied and heavy voiced, but we all knew she could and would play any role we reneged on. Last year she'd sung the role of Nathan Detroit in *Guys and Dolls* when our student Nathan lost his voice on closing night. "The orchestra will meet in here and the singers and actors will meet in the theater arts room," she boomed at us. "We'll learn the music first and then worry about the dialogue, although all of you with speaking parts should know your lines by the first of February. So be reading through them in your spare time."

Everyone laughed and poked at each other until Ms. Dalton's no-nonsense stare brought us to order. "I'll give the exact date to be off book in the next week or two. Now, rehearsals will start promptly at three on Monday, Tuesday, and Thursday—that gives you time to get a snack or whatever, but please, do not leave the school. Nobody has the time or the energy to be calling around for you. Rehearsals will be over at five. This will be our schedule for the next couple of weeks, until we see how it's going. If you goof around, we'll have more rehearsals. If you stay alert and work hard, maybe we won't take over your life."

"Huh!" Jill whispered. "I knew she was going to be a tyrant. She doesn't have a thing to do but stay here day and night. She loves it."

"Of course she does—it's her job," I said.

"It's her total reason for living, and for the next eight weeks, she's going to make it ours, too." Jill moved away, then edged back. "Let's hang out Saturday. Go to the mall. Maybe see a movie. Have some fun!"

"Okay, I'll talk to you later."

The crowd was thinning and I moved around it to my locker, where I'd left my clarinet over the Christmas break. I needed extra practice before next Monday.

"Gotta tighten up that embouchure," Peter said over my shoulder while I lifted the clarinet case out of the locker.

"You wish, Pete!" The boys behind us were hooting and laughing.

"Get lost, you guys," Peter said.

Without looking, I could hear the smile in his voice. He didn't mind a little razzing; he was enjoying his high school popularity after years of being on what, even I had to admit, was the fringes of nerddom. He hadn't had many friends in grade school—well, at least not among the guys—but in the eighth grade, he found his niche in a community theater production. On a lark, he tried out for the part of an orphan and landed the role of Oliver instead. He was good, too. His double-jointed looseness, which had kept him from being an athlete, made him a good dancer, and on the stage, a hidden grace transformed him into another person. Suddenly everybody saw him the way I always had.

"I'm glad you got Petruchio," I said, studying how one soft swatch of dark hair fell across his forehead. "You'll be great."

"I guess I can be as chauvinistic as the next guy," Peter said. "You should have tried out for a part, Annie."

"Mr. Dorsey needs me," I said, shutting my locker.

"You'd be great on the stage, though," Peter said. "You ought to get out of the pit."

He could always make me smile. "I think that's where my talents belong, thank you."

The band room was almost empty now, so we couldn't miss Ms. Dalton's resonant voice: "But surely you knew there'd be afterschool rehearsals."

She was talking to Christina Moore who had her back to us, her head bent against the director's rising tone. "Well, all I can say is you have until Monday to work something out. Otherwise, I'll have to replace you. I'm sorry, but the show's the thing here.

We all have to make a commitment."

"I've gotta go. See you later," Peter whispered, rolling his eyes toward Ms. Dalton's little scene.

I nodded and began gathering my book bag and parka. I didn't see Christina leave, but outside she was ahead of me on the walk and I hurried to catch up with her. She was still wearing just her sweater, and she huddled over her books for warmth. I stopped myself just before asking where she'd left her coat.

"Hi," I said.

"Oh, hi." Christina was watching the walk as if an obstacle might appear at any minute.

"Trouble?"

"What? Oh, I guess so." Christina gave a shuddering sigh and hugged her books more tightly. "I can't be in the show."

"Oh, gosh. I'm sorry," I said. "What's the problem?"

"I ride the bus, so I don't have a way home after practice."

"What about your folks? Can't somebody come get you?"

"My mom is a nurse practitioner over in Lawrence and she can never get away before five thirty or six, so it would be later than that before she could be here and Ms. Dalton said I can't wait at school that long. There's a rule against it."

"What about your dad?"

"He's not here right now. We moved to my grandparents' farm in November because Mom was worried about them being alone. Dad stayed in Charlotte to take care of his business, but he wants to sell it and start something here."

"And your grandparents can't drive?"

"Not at night and it's getting dark by five. I should have just told Ms. Dalton today and been done with it. Why prolong the agony? There's no way I can do it without a place to stay." Saying that much had made her breathless.

We had reached the bus lot, and I stood there while Christina disappeared on the bus. I had to squint against the glare of the afternoon sun to find her lowered head, the shadowed, dejected face. I sprinted to tap the window where she was sitting.

"What?" Christina asked over the squeak of the sliding glass.

"Don't worry, we'll think of something," I called to her. On my walk home, the perfect solution came to me.

᠑᠉

"I suppose it would be all right," Mom said. She

was whipping potatoes for dinner, and the whirl of the mixer kept interrupting us.

"The play opens the last week in February. We'll all be sick to death of it by then, but Ms. Dalton wants perfection. You know how she is." I frowned.

"I thought you liked her."

"I do." I peered into the steam of simmering pork chops. Mom had glazed them with orange marmalade just the way I liked them. "I guess I thought she was hard on Christina today, though. After all, she's new and this is the first school activity she's gone out for."

"Well, it does seem a shame for her to have to give up such a nice role," Mom said. "What's she like?"

"I don't know," I said. "I'd never even noticed her until today. I think she's really pretty, though."

"And nobody's noticed her? I'd have thought the boys would have."

"Well, she doesn't wear makeup and her clothes are kind of shabby." I paused, trying to remember. "I guess the truth is she doesn't look like us."

"Not a clone, huh?" Mom dropped a glob of butter into the steaming potatoes. "Okay, we'll check with Dad tonight just to make sure it's all right with him. You think her mother can pick her

up by six-thirty, don't you? I'd hate for this to interfere with dinner three nights a week. It's hard enough
to get us all together at the same time as it is."

"She said she could."

"Well, we could run her home now and then, if
need be," Mom said. "Surely it's not too far or she
wouldn't be at Whitney High."

Setting the table, I found myself remembering
the classroom guinea pigs and gerbils who'd
boarded with us over summer vacations. And the
strays—two kittens from a dumpster and a middle-
aged chow who had shown up on our front porch
determined to have Mom nurse him through what
turned out to be terminal cancer. Now we had
Emma Goldman, a yellow tabby we'd rescued from
the local Humane Society, and Clancy, a golden re-
triever whose unexpected appearance under the
Christmas tree five years ago had completely dis-
rupted our holiday plans. Leave it to Santa to get a
puppy for her to housebreak in the dead of winter,
Mom had said while only halfheartedly avoiding his
eager, pink-tongued licks.

"Thanks for letting Christina come, Mom."

The mixer blades clicked against the bowl.
"Don't thank me yet," she said.

But I knew it was decided.

2

The next day I watched for Christina outside Ms. Langley's English classroom. It was fourth period, so I'd already been waiting all morning, my news light and bubbly in my chest. My folks had agreed! Christina could come home with me after rehearsal. We'd have a snack—homemade oatmeal cookies, whatever fruit Mom had in the house—then we'd watch television for thirty minutes (wasn't *The Cosby Show* in reruns at that hour?) or listen to music, maybe even do homework if we had a heavy load for the next day.

Then Christina's mother would come—I could see Mom inviting her in. She'd stand in our living room in her white uniform surrounded by our color, the deep winter greens and blues of drapes and upholstery, the book-lined walls, the smoldering orange heat between the logs before Dad came in to stoke the fire. Through the archway, past the dining room, she'd glance into our kitchen, the table set with wheel-thrown pottery, the cabinets with tin fronts Mom had spent months piercing, her collection of Indian baskets decorating the walls.

And Ms. Moore, as pale and ethereal as her daughter, would smile and say how lovely it all was; she'd speak with gratitude of our family's kindness to her daughter. Maybe some nights they'd stay for supper; they'd sip the dark, rich broth of Mom's lamb stew, being revived, comforted against the cold winter night they must go out into.

We have all this to give, I thought, leaning against the wall. I didn't even bother to hide the little smile that could betray my daydream.

"What's wrong with you?" Jill asked, sliding against me.

"Nothing," I said. "Just thinking."

"That silly expression is a dead giveaway. You were all dreamy about Peter. I know it! I bet within a week you'll be driving me crazy humming 'Wunderbar.'"

"Oh, get real." Kids were pushing past us now, trying to beat the bell. "Actually, I was thinking about Christina Moore."

"What on earth for?"

"Well, after you left yesterday, I overheard her with Ms. Dalton and— Hey, Christina!" She was hurrying through the door, eyes averted from the crowd jostling around her. "Talk to you later, Jill!" I darted into the classroom behind Christina. Ms. Langley wasn't there yet, so I followed Christina to the back of the room.

"I've got it all fixed," I blurted out when she'd slipped into her desk.

"What?" She looked at me like she'd never seen me before.

"I told you I'd figure something out, remember? Well, my folks said you can come home with me after rehearsals and your mom can pick you up there." I couldn't stop beaming, although Christina was still staring at me. "So you don't have to give up the play," I went on.

"Really?" She was beginning to smile and I knew why we hadn't noticed her—she never smiled. Suddenly light came out of the shadows, her pale cheeks flushed, and she looked gorgeous.

"Meet me at lunch." I hurried to my desk just as Ms. Langley was closing the door to begin class.

An hour later, Jill and I were in the cafeteria piling toppings on our baked potatoes; then we looked for an empty table.

"I told Peter to meet us," Jill said when we'd settled near the windows.

"I told Christina, too, but I don't see her," I said.

"Christina? What's going on, Annie?" Jill poked broccoli bits into the sour cream on her potato, but she didn't begin eating.

"Yesterday I found out she couldn't be in the play because she didn't have a ride home after practice, so I asked Mom and Dad and they said she could come home with me and stay until her mom picks her up."

"You're kidding. Every afternoon?"

"It's just three afternoons a week."

Jill frowned. "Good grief, Annie, you don't even know her."

"What's to know?" I asked, digging into my potato.

"What's happening?" Peter slid into the seat beside me.

"Annie's going to play the Good Samaritan," Jill said.

"Hardly, Jill. I'm just trying to be nice to somebody who needs a favor." I turned to Peter. "Christina Moore can't be in the show unless she has a place to hang out afterward, so I've asked her to come home with me." I looked at Jill again. "Anyway, maybe she'll make some other arrangements. Maybe she'll be a lousy Lois and get replaced. Who knows what will happen?"

"My point exactly." Jill was in one of her pouts.

"I don't see what you're getting worked up about," I said. "It's hardly your business, anyway."

"Well, thank you very much." Jill studied her potato, took a bite, then pushed it away.

"Aren't you going to eat that?" Peter asked.

"Help yourself," Jill said, but she was looking at me with this hard stare she always turned on when she was really irritated with somebody. "I think I'll get a Coke and a Snickers out of the machine."

I watched her go and then dropped my fork against my plate.

"You not eating either?" Peter asked. "I know I've got a hollow leg, but I can't eat two potatoes."

"Do you think she's really peeved?"

"It's just a little attack of the greens," Peter said, crunching down on the broccoli. "You've been best friends since kindergarten or something ridiculous like that. That's longer than a lot of people stay married."

"But there's nothing for her to be jealous about. I don't want Christina for a friend—I mean, I expect we'll be friends—but she won't take Jill's place. She couldn't. Jill should know that."

"She'll get over it. Maybe she depends on you too much, anyway," Peter said. "You wanta go somewhere Saturday night? We could see that new gangster movie. Gratuitous violence always cheers you up."

I knew he was trying to make me laugh, but I wouldn't oblige him. "I told Jill I'd spend Saturday with her," I said. "That's probably what she'll want to see."

"Okay, but we've got to find time for each other, because this play is going to take every minute." He ran his fingers across my hand. "How about Sunday?"

"Okay," I said, catching his fingers, but I still couldn't give him the bright smile I knew he'd hoped for.

≥⋅

I found Christina on one of the concrete benches in front of the school where I suspected she'd eaten a bagged lunch alone. I wondered what she did on bitterly cold days or when it rained.

"Catching some rays, huh?" I sat down and

turned my face to the sun, which was a blur of white above us.

"What? Oh, yes. It's nice out here."

Every time I spoke to her, I felt like we were starting all over again. I could hear her lunch bag crackling as she squeezed it into a little ball.

"I get tired of cafeteria food, too," I said. "Sometimes I pack a lunch and eat in the band room. That's a good place when the weather's bad. And of course, you can take your—sandwich or whatever to the cafeteria. Sometimes I do that."

"It was a vegetable pita with tahini," Christina said. "I only eat fresh vegetables, mostly raw. I can't even stand the smell of that cafeteria."

So much for bologna on white, I thought. And why had I assumed that Christina's lunch would be an embarrassment in the first place? It simply hadn't occurred to me that maybe this girl had ideas I hadn't thought about, had a philosophy, for heaven's sake. It suddenly seemed possible that eating health food and sitting in the sun on winter days were part of a way of living that put Christina on a higher plane than me or my friends.

I knew I'd been acting on an old assumption anyway—one my dad had told me about from his own childhood. He'd grown up in the poor mountainous area of North Carolina where a child's status was determined by how he brought his lunch to school. Bringing it in a lard bucket was a dreadful stigma, hard to live down; a used, grease-stained paper sack was only a little improvement. Having a bread bag (proof your family could afford store-brought bread) or a crisp paper bag you could throw away put you in another class altogether, but having a real lunch box, purchased especially for that purpose, established schoolhouse royalty.

I smiled, thinking about the day my dad went to school with a shiny metal lunch box. He had been thirteen years old.

"So, you're a vegetarian," I said to Christina. "Mom used to be one, back before she got married. Then she had children and it just got simpler to roast a chicken."

"It's not for everyone," Christina agreed, and there was nothing in her tone to imply we were failures. "So, I'm going to your house after rehearsals?"

"Mom said it was okay." I tried to control my smile. "We didn't want you to have to give up such a great part."

"Oh, I hadn't given it up yet," she said.

"Well, I think this will work out fine." I stood up. "Tomorrow I'll write out directions for you to give your mother, and Monday after rehearsal we'll get together and—well, just go on home, I guess."

I surprised myself by blushing and I looked away, studying the brick school with its low roof and row of dusty windows. I didn't want Christina to know this arrangement meant a lot to me.

Why did it, anyway? I didn't really understand it. I just knew that I felt a new excitement, a tingle of expectation like you get before a holiday or a trip. Getting to know Christina Moore seemed like going to a foreign place.

Maybe it was because it had been such a long time since I'd had a new friend. I'd gone to school with the same group of kids for eleven years, beginning with kindergarten, so long there was nothing new to know about them. Peter was right about my friendship with Jill—we'd always been together. Two peas in a pod, Mom called us. The Tatums even invited me on most of their vacations, since Jill was an only child and bored without someone her own age to keep her company; she usually went camping with us, too.

And it was true we could talk in glances. Sometimes we even said the same thing at the same moment. It was neat but it was also an old routine. Lately, she seemed to irritate me too easily, and I guess she felt the same way about me, considering how she'd acted at lunch.

Then there was Peter. Ever since he'd gotten his driver's license a year ago, we'd been going out together, but we were rarely alone. Somebody in our crowd always needed a ride. Sometimes I wondered if we knew each other too well for romance, and yet there were times when, glimpsing him in the corridor at school or hearing his voice on the phone or feeling his hand against my wrist, I knew he was a person who could surprise me if he wanted to.

Those times I could hardly connect him with the awkward nine-year-old kid I'd first seen years ago whizzing by on his bike, checking out his new neighborhood. For days, Mom had been asking me to go down the street and introduce myself, but I wouldn't. Instead, I hung in the shadow of the porch watching and waiting. A week later, when he finally screeched to a stop on our walk, Mom's cake safe balanced on one hand like a waiter, I was the one to make the move. I was off the porch in a flash to have him lay the container on my open hands with a theatrical flourish that stopped my heart.

At that moment, such a quiet summer afternoon we could hear the buzz of insects in Mom's rosebushes, the whirring splash of a lawn sprinkler two yards away, we seemed to know our destiny: kids on the same street constantly thrown together at evening gatherings of our families; matinees in the downtown theater we could walk to; hours spent listening to records, memorizing lyrics and practicing dance steps on the screened-in side porch of his house. We were a perfect match.

I'd been there on opening night of *Oliver*, Jill and I squeezing each other's hands in clammy anticipation in the third row, where if he tried, Peter could see us above the lights. At Mom's suggestion, we'd sent him flowers. Boys like to get flowers, too, she'd said, and sprung for the five dollars that got us two yellow roses in a milk-glass bud vase, which the florist delivered to the little theater minutes before the opening curtain.

"These must be Peter's admirers," a dusty, T-shirted Fagan had teased when we found ourselves backstage in the communal dressing room after the performance, costumes swishing onto racks, fluffs of tissues floating toward wastebaskets, pink sweaty faces appearing from under stiff wigs and heavy makeup.

And he hadn't been embarrassed. Not Peter, who hugged us simultaneously, the three of us linked in a crushing embrace in the middle of the crowded room. Oh, I loved him that night!

And then there were all the days I stood with him in an open field while he trained his first sparrow hawk, my eyes closed to the flapping lift from the glove. I was wary of the birds, although I'd helped him make lures and clean the mews his dad had built beside the garage in their yard. Sometimes I even carried a hooded hawk on my fist, feeling the talons' fierce grip just short of an ache in my hand.

Over the years, we'd also spent time in each other's rooms—his was a book-strewn garret he never bothered to tidy, where I'd lie on his bed reading while he practiced his guitar, the chords lulling me into a doze until he'd start playing something I loved, "Round Midnight" maybe, or "Vincent." His room might stay the same, but he'd seen mine change several times: Barbies replaced with books and tapes, silly animal posters ripped down for Greenpeace whales and a grungy Michael Stipe in front of REM. But did he truly see how I was changing, how I wanted him to feel passionately about me? Could I ever be new to him, someone he'd desperately want to touch, kiss, whisper to? He'd taken my refusal for Saturday night so easily, as if I were just one of his possibilities.

"Annie," someone was calling to me. "Annie, the

first bell just rang." It was Christina.

I stirred and stood up, stretching. "Oh yeah. Biology, yuck. What do you have now?"

"French," Christina said as we pushed through the glass door into the lobby.

"Why aren't you in my class?" I asked.

"I'm in the third level. I took French in junior high. *Au revoir.*"

I was almost late, so Jill was already at our lab table, her book open in front of her. "Where've you been?" she wanted to know. "I looked everywhere."

"I went outside—it's a beautiful day." I opened my book without looking at her.

"I wanted to say I'm sorry"—Jill whispered because Ms. Martinez was rapping her desk for attention—"about what happened at lunch."

"Me too," I mouthed, grateful that Ms. Martinez was beginning on time. I couldn't remember when Jill and I had needed to apologize to each other. I felt my empty stomach flutter, my mouth go dry, knowing that the awkwardness between us was only part of the problem. I didn't want Jill to know I'd been with Christina.

"Either you're in his face or he's oblivious." I laughed.

The back door suddenly pushed open and Mom, hidden behind two grocery bags, maneuvered in before I could move to help her. She deposited the sacks on the counter and peeled off her gloves with a weary sigh.

"Is that it?" I asked.

"Oh hi, girls." She smiled at us. "Martha's getting the other one. Sometimes I feel like I live in the produce department." She started emptying one of the bags, then stopped to slip out of her jacket.

"Greg's eating us out of house and home," I said to explain the giant jar of peanut butter and two jugs of milk on the counter. "Mom, this is Christina."

"Well, I knew it must be. Hello, dear. It's nice to meet you finally. Annie's been so—"

I was relieved when the door opened again before Mom could say how excited I'd been, and there was my little sister, tottering under the weight of an unwieldy load. "This was the heavy one," Martha complained breathlessly. "Mom, they put every single can in this bag."

"Well, why don't you go down and offer bag-boy training?" I helped her settle the sack on the table. "Martha's the impatient one around here."

"I am not. I just don't see why people can't think now and then." She brightened. "Oh, hi! You're Christina. You got the part of Lois, didn't you? I love that part. Last year I wanted to sing 'Always True to You' in the school talent show, but old Ms. Etheridge—she's our music teacher—said it was inappropriate." Martha rolled her eyes in disgust.

"What did you do instead?" Christina asked.

"Oh, some old thing that's been done a thousand times. We can't get away with anything at my school. My friend Michelle sang 'Material Girl' at auditions, and Ms. Etheridge practically wouldn't let her perform at all because of it. Ms. Etheridge is an old priss."

"I could help you find a song for this year," Christina said, finally smiling. I could see she was beginning to relax a little. "I have lots of music at home. We could find a sure winner."

"That's great!" Martha said. "Mom, did you hear? Christina's going to help me."

"Why, I thought 'I'm Just a Girl Who Can't Say No' was perfect for you," I teased.

"Anne Gerhardt, don't bait her!" Mom said, laughing. She was putting the groceries away, and the cabinets swung open and shut like a little chorus behind her. "Martha, help me get this stuff cleared away so I can get supper started. Dad'll be home any minute."

"Why can't Annie?"

"Annie has a guest."

"Besides, you're twelve and a peon, right, Mom?" I got up and motioned for Christina to follow.

"I am not!" Martha flung her jacket at me. "Mom, what's a peon?"

"A servant. A person working off a debt. You owe us because you're adopted," Greg said from the doorway. He was damp and shiny and the smell of shampoo hovered around him.

"Greg, don't tell her that!" Mom said. "Sometimes I wonder about these people," she went on to Christina. "Maybe they're all three aliens, although I remember three specific labors, especially yours, sweetheart." She gave Martha a quick hug. "Because you were the easiest."

"See!" Martha looked smug.

"We're going to watch television," I said, "while you stay here and slave."

"We could help with dinner," Christina offered. "I'd like to."

"Bless your heart. Why don't I take you up on that some other time?" Mom smiled at her and then lifted a saucepan off the hook above the stove. "Tonight you're still company. Besides, your mother should be here any minute."

"Sometimes she may be late," Christina said. "She's a nurse practitioner for Dr. Winston over in Lawrence, and she has to stay until the very last patient leaves." Her voice quavered as if saying so much were an effort for her.

"Well, it can't be too long, can it?" Mom said agreeably. "And we'll run you home some nights, if need be. Greg can do that, can't you?"

"Sure." Greg was getting a pear out of a sack.

"Now everybody scoot," Mom said, "and let me get cooking."

Dad was home and dinner was waiting when the bell rang and Mom opened the door to a tall, frowning woman wearing a bright-red coat over her white slacks.

"Ms. Gerhardt?" the woman said, stepping over the threshold. She stood in the foyer, the door open behind her, and slapped her gloves against her hand. "I'm Danice Moore. I believe my daughter's here."

"She certainly is, and please call me Eleanor. Here's Christina now," Mom said, because Christina had heard and was heading for the foyer, tugging on her coat as she went. "Can you come in for a minute?"

"I left the car running," Ms. Moore said.

"Oops, I forgot my books." Christina started back to the kitchen.

"Well, hurry. I didn't tell the folks I'd be late."

"You could call from here," Mom offered.

"It's okay, if Christina will just get a move on." Ms. Moore swept around, about to disappear in the dark beyond the porch light.

"Mama, wait a minute. I want you to meet Annie," Christina called after her.

"Hi," the woman said, hardly glancing back at me.

"See you tomorrow," Christina said, her voice fading in a gust of cold around us.

"Goodness, what was that?" Mom asked when she'd closed the door behind them.

Not what I expected, I thought, following her into the kitchen where the rest of the family had gathered for dinner. It looked like Christina had a bulldozer for a mother, which was all the more reason why I should be her friend. Tomorrow I'd describe the scene to Jill and then she'd be sympathetic, too. I'd make her understand how much Christina needed us both.

❧

On Wednesdays after school, Jill and I had drivers' ed. with Mr. Andrews, whom years ago students had nicknamed Andretti. Pale and humorless, he folded himself into the mid-size Chevrolet every afternoon as if he were being sealed in a tomb and said little to the students as they drove except to bark warnings when they threatened his life by straying too close to the centerline or entered the flow of traffic at the wrong speed.

Today we were scheduled to parallel park, and so on Saturday afternoon we had practiced in the driveway between two garbage cans while Greg gave us advice between convulsions of laughter at how uncoordinated we both were.

Now we hurried across the parking lot to meet Mr. Andrews and Dan Coleman, the other student in our group. "I'm telling you, I can't do it!" Jill was saying. "I'll be on the curb! God, I'll probably jump the curb and end up in a storefront! It'll be in the newspaper!"

"I don't see how you can ski and play volleyball and dance and not be able to steer a car backward," I said.

"It's not me! It's Andretti! He makes me so nervous I could die. And Dan in the backseat! He'll razz me forever if I mess up even a little bit!"

"Well, you've been wanting him to notice you,"

I said. "Maybe he can't park either."

"Oh, he can! He was driving his dad's truck before he could see over the steering wheel. He even drives on the highway out near their farm. He told me so."

"You'll do fine," I whispered. "Just pretend there's nobody in the car but you and me."

"I wish," Jill said, then smiled brightly at the sour-looking man waiting beside the car. "Hi!" she said. "Sorry if we're late." We crawled into the backseat without waiting for him to respond.

Mr. Andrews motioned to Dan, who popped behind the wheel. "I see parallel parking is on the schedule for today," he said, getting in. He studied the sheet on his clipboard. "Head on downtown, Dan. If you people can't park in traffic, you may as well not know how to park at all."

"Jeez." Jill grimaced and squeezed my hand so tightly I had to pull away. "I bet I could go the rest of my life not parking parallel," she whispered.

"Yeah, you could spend it circling." I giggled softly.

"The secret to parallel parking is the position of the car before you begin to enter the space," Mr. Andrews was droning, oblivious of our giggles. "It's crucial that you properly line up your vehicle with the vehicle in the space in front of you. The next important point is when to start turning the wheel. That's something you learn with practice, although the rule is: Turn when the front passenger door is parallel with the bumper of the vehicle beside you."

"What if it's a two-door vehicle?" Jill squeaked from the back. She couldn't resist being noticed even when she claimed otherwise. "Or a sports car?"

"If one of the vehicles is a sports car, you have an advantage, don't you? A smaller car in the space will make maneuvering easier." Mr. Andrews answered as if Jill were serious.

We laughed soundlessly and even Dan, who was concentrating on the road, grinned at us through the rearview mirror.

"Here," Mr. Andrews said, because we were on Main Street now. "Here's a nice empty spot." It was between a jacked-up truck and an old Lincoln. Dan pulled up close to the truck in front and whipped the car backward into the space. He waited, the car purring under us.

"Very good. Now pull out so Jill can have a try," Mr. Andrews said without much enthusiasm.

"Mr. Andrews, I haven't gotten to practice much," Jill started.

"This is practice," he said sternly. "Now come on up here."

Jill and I exchanged pained looks before she

took Dan's place in the driver's seat. She rubbed her hands on the steering wheel, waiting. The heater was blasting enough heat to make me shed my coat in the back.

"It's awfully hot in here," Jill said.

Mr. Andrews flipped the heater switch to a lower setting, but the warm air continued to blow. I was feeling damp under my clothes, and there was a trickle of perspiration down Jill's temple.

"Now see how Dan left you lined up with the truck. All you have to do is back into the space just like he came out of it." Mr. Andrews was watching through his side mirror. "Now start backing, slow and easy.

"Now don't start turning too soon," Mr. Andrews went on. "If you do, you'll clip the truck or your back tires will hit the curb."

"Either way, you're dead," Dan said. He was laughing under his voice.

"Sh-h-h-h," Mr. Andrews said. "Concentration, that's the key. Nobody's here but you. And me."

Jill didn't say anything. I could see her craning her head to get a look at me in the rearview mirror, so I looked out the window, trying not to distract her. The tires and bumper on the truck beside us looked gigantic.

"Mr. Andrews, I don't think I'm ready for this," Jill said, pressing the brake hard.

"One more class in this section of drivers' ed., Jill. If you don't park today, you won't get your permit."

"Oh-h-h," she moaned, and eased down on the accelerator. The car barely moving, she inched backward, angling the car slightly. I watched the truck tire passing so close I could smell the rubber. It seemed like hours in slow motion while traffic stopped behind us, the other drivers heeding the flashing caution lights on top of the car. Finally, we were parallel, the tires tight against the curb, the rear bumper pressed to the nose of the Lincoln.

"Now," Mr. Andrews said loudly, as if he'd just accomplished a great feat, "get out."

Before I could reach forward to stop her, Jill had burst out like an animal let loose and slammed the door behind her. She seemed to be standing at attention on the sidewalk, waiting for whatever orders would come next.

"Good grief," Mr. Andrews said, rolling down the window. "Jill, I meant get out of the parking space."

êa

"You mean she got out of the car?" Christina said. We were walking home from rehearsal on Thursday. "She actually did that!" Christina bent forward laughing, her breath coming in frosty gusts.

"Well, she was nervous. People do things like that when they're nervous," I said, walking on in front of her. "Anyhow, it's not that funny."

"It's dumb, that's what," Christina said, catching up.

And I hurried along, suddenly burdened with a quick knot of regret in my chest. I wished I hadn't told.

4

Ms. Langley brought our English class to order with a question. "Your country has recently elected a new president who has turned out to be a dictator. In his quest for personal power, he is destroying the system by which your country has operated successfully for years. What would you be willing to do to stop him?"

Nobody responded, so Ms. Langley waited, surveying the room of blank faces until someone finally spoke from the back. "I'd get a gun and shoot him," the voice said softly.

The entire front half of class turned almost simultaneously to identify the assassin. I knew without looking it was Christina.

"You'd kill him?" Ms. Langley asked, barely concealing her surprise.

"Well, I probably wouldn't do it myself. I guess I'd hire somebody," Christina said. Her voice was quavery but she sounded determined.

"She'd hire Ernie," Dan said, and the rest of the guys hooted with laughter. "He's the best shot in here. Aren't you, Ernie?"

"That ain't saying much," Ernie mumbled.

"You'd do it, man. You'd blow him away!"

Ernie came out of his slouch. It was probably the first time English class had interested him all year. "I don't know as I'd be wanting to shoot a person," he said slowly. "My uncle Ernest D. was in Vietnam and he shot a lot of Cong. After that he couldn't sleep good and his wife left him." He slid back down in his desk, looking embarrassed by all he'd revealed.

"So you wouldn't kill this man?" Ms. Langley asked. "You wouldn't take say, five thousand dollars from Christina and eliminate this power-hungry dictator?"

"He'd do it!" Eric Sanders said. "Ernie, come on, man. For five G's, you'd do anything."

"Five G's ain't that much money," Ernie mumbled. "You want him dead, you do it."

"Then let's look at the question differently," Ms. Langley said. "Let's assume Christina doesn't have any money but she does have a good cause. She wants her country rid of this man who is destroying her way of life, someone who is abusing power, someone who is already so strong he can't be removed by the usual political process."

"Out in the Old West they would have lynched him," Dan said. "A mob would have done it. Or they'd have a shoot-out."

"What about these coups in all those little countries? The military takes over the government," Jill said. "Imagine, the Pentagon in charge of the United States!" She faked a shiver.

"My dad thinks it already is in charge," I said.

"Most of the time military coups don't work, though. The generals are as bad as the scumbag dictator was," one of the boys offered.

"I don't think we should ever kill another person," Phoebe Hahn said adamantly. Jill and I smiled. Phoebe was always on a soapbox. "I don't think we should even have the death penalty."

"You want Ted Bundy walking around?" Dan asked.

"No, but killing him didn't bring those women back."

"You couldn't lock up a dictator, could you, and keep him there?" one of the boys said. "If he was strong enough, he'd have influence even from prison like those Mafia guys do. Nothing changes when they go to jail."

"So I guess we'd have to get together and kill him," Dan said. "All of us."

"Then you're saying that there are times when the end justifies the means?" Ms. Langley asked. "It's all right to take immoral action, even commit murder, for a moral cause?"

"Huh?" Ernie squirmed. "Say what?"

We were silent again and Ms. Langley waited while we pretended to think it over.

It was Christina who finally broke the silence. "Does this mean we're reading *Julius Caesar* next?" she asked.

"Shakespeare! Barf!" we moaned. We were still grousing when the bell rang.

અ

On Saturday afternoon, I stood on the edge of an open field. It was warm for January, the sky sunny in mid-afternoon although the brown weeds still held dampness after a powdering of snow two days before. I moved my feet in my sneakers, feeling the ground cold invading my socks. It wouldn't be long before my feet were soaked.

Peter's red-tailed hawk was circling above me,

but mostly I watched Peter who waited in the center of the field, immobile but watchful himself. I could tell that he was soaring with the bird. I knew how he let his mind go, made himself weightless, so light he felt airborne with the hawk. I couldn't help but smile at the picture they made.

"You want to bring her in?" Peter called to me, but I shook my head. When he'd phoned earlier to ask if I could come with him this afternoon, he'd said we wouldn't be long—an hour or so because he wasn't hunting the red-tail, just letting her fly. "Since it gets dark so early and I've got rehearsal, Dad's been taking her out," he explained, "but I promised him I'd fly her at least once every weekend until she molts."

Of course we were already deep into the second hour, but I hadn't complained. I could see how Peter loved it. I watched him swing the lure—it was an old one I'd help make, and I remembered how the flat end of the needle had dug into my fingers when I'd pushed it through the leather bird we'd sewn, how we'd stitched bright feathers to it. The lure whipped the air, and I would have thought it was whistling had I not known the sound Peter could make between his teeth. Above him, Rosie hovered for a moment, then swooped down, coming in for the kill. She caught the lure low and brought it down, wings back, her golden breast and bright belly bands exposed. Then she settled over the bit of meat Peter had tied to the lure.

"What an act, Rosie." I stepped around rocks and stumps getting to them. "She's such a show-off."

"Yeah. She was today." Peter didn't try to hide the pleasure in his voice. "Dad said when he brought her out Thursday, she perched in that pine tree over there for thirty minutes, but it was cold and cloudy that day, wasn't it, Rosie? You know when to fly, don't you, girl?" The hawk had finished the meat, so he put his hand behind her legs and she stepped onto the glove. "Will you get the perch?"

I pulled the metal ring out of the ground and collected the lure while Peter attached the leash to Rosie's jesses.

"After I get her in, you want to grab something to eat?"

"As long as it's not a chicken neck."

"We won't eat with Rosie," Peter said. "Besides, you don't like to share, do you, girl? We'll get a burger or something."

The hawk watched us patiently, as if she were weary of our chatter but indulgent, too. She fluttered slightly on the fist, settling herself.

Peter locked the perch between the seats of the Jeep. Unhooded, Rosie moved her head back and forth, watching us until the Jeep was moving smoothly on the highway.

"I didn't think you'd come today," Peter said. "You and Jill always have plans before I can figure out what's happening."

"Sure. You're so-o-o busy." I pulled off my wet shoes.

"So are you. School, the play, and now this new girl," Peter said.

"Not you, too." I leaned back, propping my damp sock-feet on the dash.

"So Jill still doesn't like her, huh?"

"Not really, but I guess she'll come around. I don't know what the big deal is."

"I've already told you, Annie. She's jealous." Peter turned the Jeep into his driveway and stopped. "And I know the feeling."

"You? Jealous? Of what? Of who?"

"Well, when I was a kid, I wanted to be good at sports and I envied guys who were. I guess I'm over that, not that I still wouldn't like to throw a fifty-yard pass."

"But you never acted like you cared. I thought you were always into birds."

"Sure. I liked going out with Dad—it was something we could do together—so he helped me train that first sparrow hawk. Then I got Rosie here." The hawk cocked her head, listening to him.

Peter turned off the engine, pulled on his glove and put his fist behind the bird's feet. She stepped on. He waited a moment before getting out. "I didn't let on I cared about a lot of things when we were kids. I mean, it was you and Jill and me all the time and that was fine. Now I wish she'd bug out or at least get a boyfriend. I just want to be with you, Annie."

I didn't say anything. It was what I wanted to hear, and yet it didn't seem quite real, like a good dream you feel yourself forgetting too soon.

I watched him disappear into the mews with the bird. Between the vertical slats, I could see the quick flap of wings as Rosie was released to fly to her favorite perch near the ceiling. I knew Peter was putting out meat for her dinner—the haunch of a squirrel saved from a previous hunt, a road-kill opossum he'd salvaged. I didn't want to watch, so I leaned back with my eyes closed, feeling the dusky air chilling around me.

"I need to wash up before we go," Peter said through the window. "You want to come in a minute?"

I shook my head and he disappeared into the house. I just want to be with you, he'd said. I'll hold on to that, I thought as I waited in the growing dark. I watched the lights in his house, knowing how it looked in every room, around the corners hidden from me now, up the stairwell at the center. I saw his light go on upstairs.

But what about Jill, though? She was spending the weekend at her parents' condo at Pine Knoll Shores. I could be there with her right now. We could be walking on the beach, the wind whipping under our jackets, the surf rolling toward us with its cold winter roar we'd have to shout over.

When she invited me, I knew she wanted to use the weekend to make sure things were okay between us, but I made up a lame excuse that ended up making Mom the villain. Why did I do that?

It wasn't that I didn't want to be with her. I just wanted to be at home. That was all. I wanted to sleep late and make pancakes for lunch and listen to music while I attacked the mess in my room. I wanted to hear Martha and her sleep-over friend giggling in her room, to find Greg half asleep on the sofa while a basketball game made bright colors on the TV screen. I wanted to see Mom and Dad there, too, taking a nap on their bed with the door open, Mom's head on Dad's chest, his hand on her hair as if they'd fallen to sleep mid-stroke. Until Peter called, I thought I wanted to be alone.

He opened the door, jarring me awake. The air around my ankles was cool, then suddenly warm, and I shivered with it.

"Food then," Peter said.

"Uh-huh." I leaned over quickly to kiss him on the cheek.

"What's that for?" he asked.

"No reason," I said.

"Well hey, I've got enough reasons for both of us," he said, and pulled me into his arms.

ॐ

Jill came over as soon as she got home on Sunday.

"So what did you do?" she asked, pushing my books out of the way so she could lie down on the bed.

"Worked on our biology project, for one thing," I said. We were supposed to be collaborating but Jill hadn't started her part yet.

"I know, I know." She rolled over to stare at the ceiling. "I'll do it this week, I promise. So what did you do that was fun?"

"Nothing. I cleaned up. Can't you tell?"

"Annie, give me a break, okay? What did you and Peter do?"

"Flew Rosie."

"And?"

"A pizza at Giovanni's." I stretched out on the other bed. "Dan was there."

"Who was he with? Jeez, I knew I should have stayed home! Who wants to go to the beach in the dead of winter, anyway?" She flopped back onto her stomach and buried her head under a pillow. "Okay, tell me. Who was he with?"

"I don't even remember. Eric. Phoebe. A gang of people. They were going to the movies afterward."

"And you and Peter didn't go with them?"

"Nope. We rented a movie and watched it here."

"Alone, huh? You guys!" Jill hugged the pillow. "Let me guess—*Out of Africa* for the umpteenth time?"

"*Henry the Fifth*, with Martha between us," I said.

"You two are so boring!" Jill bounced up. "Hey, I smell popcorn!"

Dad was in the kitchen, turning the popcorn out into a gigantic bowl. "This is for the game," he said, cradling the bowl protectively in his arm. "You've got to watch the Redskins if you want some."

"He's kidding," I said. "He doesn't even want us in there. We ask dumb questions."

"Not true. But you two do have a tendency to start yakking on the most crucial plays." Dad poured popcorn into another bowl for us. Then he got two cans of soda out of the fridge. "Now leave us be," he said. "Greg and I have some male bonding to do."

"And it won't be a pretty sight," Mom said, coming in. She grabbed a handful of popcorn as Dad passed by. "So how's the play coming along, girls?"

"Terrible!" Jill said. "It's just awful."

She and Mom sat down at the kitchen table while I got sodas.

"I think it's fine. You know your song," I said. "Peter knows most of his—of course, he's got a lot to learn. Christina knows hers, too."

"Well, of course she does." Jill dug into the popcorn. "She wants to impress everybody."

Mom gave me a quizzical look but I kept on munching. I hadn't told her that Jill didn't like Christina's coming home with me.

"Well, I think Christina's a lovely girl," Mom said.

"Yeah," Jill said. "She's okay."

So she doesn't want to admit she's jealous, I thought. Or maybe she's beginning to realize she's been unreasonable.

"Catch," I said, tossing a piece of popcorn at her. She tried to catch it on her tongue but missed.

"Again," she said and missed.

"You two are going to have popcorn all over the floor," Mom warned us.

"One more time," Jill said. This time she caught it and crunched down with a grin.

I smiled back at her. We were going to be okay.

5

Since Mr. Dorsey was using the piano to teach the singers the score to *Kiss Me, Kate*, he could rehearse with the orchestra only two afternoons a week. Ms. Dalton, never one to ignore idle hands, put me on the construction crew building the flats that would eventually frame the Italian piazza in the show.

"I'm sure you have hidden talent," Ms. Dalton said matter-of-factly. I knew it was because Dad taught industrial technology at the university.

For once I felt sympathy for Greg, who was expected to make wonderful birdhouses and bookends in Boy Scouts and who transferred out of freshman shop two weeks into the school year with a broken thumb and a wobbly footstool he dropped in the trash. His thumb was still painful when basketball try-outs were held, but he managed to get on the J.V. team. That summer he started the growth spurt that made him Whitney High's star forward by his junior year. Now all he cared about was basketball.

I didn't have something to die for like that. I was successful at most everything I tried, but then, I didn't attempt anything especially challenging. I was in the right crowd and I made good grades without much effort. I guess I didn't think much about myself. A car and a summer job were at the top of my wish list, and I figured I'd get the car because Dad had bought Greg one. Precedent had been set, the great advantage of being the second child.

I already had a couple of leads on summer jobs, too. The one I really wanted was working with the groomer at a boarding kennel, but if that didn't work out, there were always the fast-food places. I was glad my folks wouldn't allow us to have after-school or weekend jobs during the school year.

"Studying is your job right now," Dad said, "so enjoy it." He'd bought Greg that old Toyota to prove he was serious about our putting school before car payments, so from my point of view, wheels were a *fait accompli*.

Walking home after Tuesday's rehearsal, I told

Jill and Christina about my set-building assignment.

"I think you should have refused." Jill was adamant. "That's the shop students' job."

"Oh, it's all right. Maybe I'll learn something."

Christina said, "I worked on set construction at my school in Charlotte. Everybody in the cast helped. It was interesting, too. Do you know if you use white paint on a set, you have to speckle it with a dark color, otherwise it glares so bright the audience can't look at it?"

"Of course we knew that," Jill said. We had stopped at the edge of my walk.

"I didn't." I smiled at Christina. "I hope we've got food. I'm starving. You want to come in, Jill?"

"No thanks. I need lots of time to get ready for tonight."

"Jill met this guy named Drew when we played at Lawrence High before Christmas," I explained to Christina.

"We met in the line at the concession stand. I actually gave him my phone number, but he never called," Jill said "I know he'll be at the game tonight, though. I just know it."

"I thought you liked Dan," Christina said.

"Who told you that?" Jill wanted to know. "You

54

did!" She gave me a playful punch on the arm that sank through my sleeve.

"Everybody knows it," Christina said.

"Except maybe Dan," I said. "So what are you wearing tonight?"

"Shades of white and beige," Jill said. "What do you think? I've got these new beige stirrup pants and that off-white sweater and my boots. How about you?"

"I'm wearing jeans. We always wear jeans."

"Well, don't tonight, Annie! Come on and dress up so I won't look like I'm too much!" Jill turned to Christina. "Get her to dress up! This may be the only time I see him all winter."

"I'm not going to the game," Christina said.

"Well, you could!" I said. "Let's call your mom and ask her to pick you up afterward."

"She wouldn't," Christina said. "Once she's home, she doesn't want to go out again."

"Well, maybe Dad could take you home." Suddenly it seemed terribly unfair for Christina to be left out of our plans.

"Annie—" Jill started, but I wouldn't let her stop me.

"Or you could spend the night! You could wear a shirt of Martha's. You're about the same size. Or something of mine. Between us, we have plenty you can wear."

Jill finally said irritably, "I wanted both of us to dress up, remember?"

"Well, you can. You'll look great." My attention was still on Christina.

"Mom might let me stay," she said, giving me a smile, "if your mother calls her." It was amazing to see her face light up.

"Done!" I said. "Jill, we'll meet you at the game."

Greg didn't come to the table.

"He left an hour ago, so Christina, you can take his place," Mom said.

We were having baked chicken with mushroom sauce, but Christina could eat the rice, broccoli, and salad that went with it.

"Doesn't Greg eat before a game?" she wanted to know after Dad had said the blessing and the food was being passed.

"No," he said. "On game days he eats mid-afternoon and then is as hungry as a horse afterward. We should all eat afterward, I suppose. We get pretty excited about basketball."

"But you don't yell at the referees like some dads do," Martha said.

"No, I don't," Dad said. "Harrassment never changed a call yet that I know of."

"Do you like sports?" Mom asked Christina, who was nibbling at her salad.

"Not much." She gave Mom a shy smile. "If my brother hadn't got leukemia, I'm sure he would have played basketball, though. I would have watched him every game."

"Oh, my. I'm—we're so sorry," Mom said gently and reached over to squeeze Christina's hand.

"I don't know what I'd do without Greg and Annie," Martha said. She'd put her fork down and was looking mournfully at Christina as if she could find some preventive in her face. "They pick on me all the time, but I'm used to it. I like it."

"I'll remember that, peon," I said, forcing a laugh. I didn't know how to tell Christina how sorry I was about her brother.

"So what's happening at school?" Dad asked.

"We started *Julius Caesar* in English this week." I was grateful to have the subject changed.

"So how's it going?" Mom wanted to know.

"Okay, I guess. Looks pretty boring to me."

"Do you like Shakespeare, Christina?" Dad asked.

"I liked *Romeo and Juliet* last year," Christina said.

"That's the one I want to read," Martha said. "I

saw the movie, and even with them talking funny, it was so romantic and sad."

"Yesterday Ms. Langley told us about the Elizabethan period, the theater companies, and all that," Christina said. "Tomorrow she's telling us about Shakespeare himself. She talks a lot."

"Same old stuff, too," I added. "Stratford-on-Avon and all that."

"Anne Hathaway's cottage," Martha put in knowingly, then gave Christina a conspiratorial look. "We don't believe it."

"Don't believe what?" Christina put her fork down.

"That the man who lived in Stratford wrote the plays," I said. "Mom's the one really into it, though."

"We just go along to keep peace," Dad said, taking another roll from the basket.

"Who wrote them then?" Christina wanted to know.

"That's the mystery." Mom smiled. "It just bothered me in college that this man from Stratford who could barely write his name—you know he even spelled it differently in the few signatures we have—managed to have the background, the education, mind you, to produce all those great plays."

"But he was a genius, wasn't he?" Christina said.

"Very good!" Mom said. "That's one of the arguments—that genius can spring from nowhere. I just don't happen to believe it."

"You ought to bring it up in class, Annie," Christina said. "Tell Ms. Langley."

"Let's just keep this to ourselves," Dad said. "Greg mentioned it in Carl Johnson's class a couple of years ago and got shot down, nearly a mortal wound."

"He got a D for the unit," I explained, "but that's how Mr. Johnson is. Besides, Greg argued the point on his final exam—how there's no indication the man from Stratford read well enough to know Roman history—and that wasn't even one of the questions."

"I bet Ms. Langley would listen," Christina said.

"Well then, Annie, 'into the breach.'" Mom brandished her fork with a laugh.

"No way." I frowned at the thought. "I've got enough on my plate."

❧

At the gym, Christina and I waited in the corridor for Jill. The game was starting when she finally arrived, as bright as new metal against our dark winter clothes.

"Now I feel like an idiot," she said, huddling

between us. "He's probably not here anyway."

"Aren't we going to watch the game?" Christina asked. We could hear the National Anthem, a staticky recording of the marching band. "I want to see Greg play."

"You know Amanda Pickens wants Greg to take her to the Spring Fling, don't you?" Jill told me. "Everybody in the school knows it by now. I heard she said if he didn't ask her soon, she was going to go with a college boy. She'd do it, too."

"If she's so hot, why is she giving Greg ultimatums?" Christina wanted to know.

"I haven't the foggiest idea."

Jill was peering beyond us, scanning the hall. "I wish Drew would show up!"

"Maybe he's watching the game," Christina suggested.

"Of course he isn't. We don't come to watch the game. We come to see who else comes," Jill said, unable to hide her exasperation.

"Isn't that him?" I asked.

"Where?" Jill was jiggling between us. "Don't look! Just tell me, right or left."

"Your left. He's coming toward us right now," I whispered.

Jill peeped around Christina to see. "It's him.

Oh, God, he's here, and I'm not ready!"

"I'm going inside," I said. "You coming, Christina?"

"No! Stay here with me!" Jill pressed against the wall as if she could disappear into it, while we moved away from her, heading for the gym.

I stopped at the doorway and looked back just in time to see Jill move out into the corridor, her boots clicking, face tortured around a funny little smile, to confront the man of her dreams.

Drew was just two feet from her when I heard her greet him. "Hi, Jill," she said.

He nodded and went past while she turned to us, her face as white as her sweater before a pink blush blossomed on her cheeks.

"I said 'Hi, Jill,'" she cried, falling into my arms. "He didn't even know I was talking to him. He didn't even see me."

"I think that's just as well," Christina said. She wasn't even trying to control her smile.

"There'll be another time," I said.

"I just want to die," Jill moaned.

"The score's already eight to twelve," Christina said.

"Like I care!" Jill pulled away and stared at us. "Nobody cares about me, that's for sure. I just had the most humiliating experience of my life and you two—" She stopped, her golden hair shimmering around her pink face. "You two are laughing! Why are you laughing?"

"Because—" I gasped over the bubble of laughter that was exploding in my throat, "because it was so funny!"

I pressed my hands over my mouth, trying to control myself. Christina was bent double.

"Well, I guess it was," Jill said, still trying not to smile. "Just don't you tell a soul. I mean it. I don't want to hear about this—not ever."

But later during halftime when Jill came out of the stall in the girls' room, Christina and I were standing there, arms linked to greet her. "Hi, Jill!" we cried in unison, and the three of us fell against each other, laughing again.

6

On Thursday, after spending the first twenty minutes of English class talking about Roman government, customs, and dress, Ms. Langley reminded us that the story itself, particularly the assassination plot, could take place anytime, anywhere.

"Not with names like Brutus and Flavius," Jill interjected.

"I bet there are guys in Italy named that," Dan Coleman said, grinning as he always did when he saw a chance to irritate her. They were like two sparks working on a flame. "If you lived in Rome, you'd probably be dating a Brutus and Cassius. He thumbed through the pages. "How about Clitus?"

The boys snickered and Jill turned away haughtily, which meant she was on the verge of embarrassment.

"There's one named that, I swear. There is, isn't there, Ms. Langley?" Dan was at the point of blushing himself.

"You're right, Dan, and when we get to that scene, you can tell us all about him," Ms. Langley said, holding back a smile. She closed her book and leaned against her desk. "Now let's talk a moment about how Shakespeare might have come upon this story. Does anybody know where it was recorded?"

Nobody moved.

"Ernie?"

"Huh? Did we have to read that?" He flipped open his book, but he wasn't even close to the right section.

"It was in the text notes, but no, I didn't specifically assign it," Ms. Langley said, undaunted.

"Well, I dunno then," Ernie said and went back to filling in the O's on the front of his composition book.

"Christina?" She must have raised her hand from the back.

"I think it's in Plutarch's *Lives*, but Ms. Langley, wouldn't Shakespeare have had to be an educated person to know about that?" Her voice was shivery, but I could hear the pulse in it.

What's she doing? I wondered, and looked at

Jill, who was rolling her eyes like she wasn't at all surprised.

"Well, it's true he probably had only a grammar-school education, but scholars believe such an education was the equivalent of our college degree," Ms. Langley said with a confident smile.

"Some people think he couldn't even spell his name," Christina went on breathlessly. "Annie's mother, for instance. She doesn't believe he wrote anything at all."

Everybody was paying attention now.

"Well, Annie, tell us about it," Ms. Langley said cheerfully.

"I don't know much. It's something Mom's been interested in for a long time. It's just an idea." I was struggling not to sound peeved. Ms. Langley was still smiling.

"Hair-brained, if you ask me," Dan said. "I guess she thinks a woman wrote all that stuff."

This was just what I had expected. I turned to face the class. "No. But she does believe an educated person wrote them, and so do I!"

"How interesting!" Ms. Langley said eagerly over the bell. "Read Scene Two for tomorrow, and we'll talk more about the authorship question as well."

At the last bell, I went straight to the theater arts room to play the piano accompaniment for the fifth scene of *Kiss Me, Kate*.

"Take them through 'Tom, Dick, or Harry' several times," Ms. Dalton had said that morning. "Nobody's coming in at the right time. Except Christina, that is."

At the time I'd been glad to get off the set crew for the afternoon, but now I just wanted to go home. Since English class I'd felt out of sorts, and I didn't want to see anybody, especially not Christina. Of course, that business in English class wasn't completely her fault. Obviously, I should have told her specifically not to mention the Shakespeare question instead of just assuming she'd know better.

She came in with a soft-drink can balanced on top of her books.

"I thought you didn't put junk in your body." Surprised by the icy tone in my voice, I struck a dissonant bass chord for cover.

"It's ten percent real orange juice," she read off the label. "The best I can do around here." She put her books on a chair, then snapped the can open and offered it to me.

"No thanks. I'll poison myself later."

Christina didn't seem to notice how impatient I sounded. She sat down on the bench next to me. "So, where are the guys?"

"I haven't the slightest idea." I pounded out several chords.

"What's wrong, Annie?" Christina put the can on the edge of the piano and began fingering the soprano notes in the upper register.

"Nothing." I couldn't look at her. "I didn't know you play the piano."

"A little." She was jazzing up the melody, adding little riffs.

"A little better than me, for sure. Why don't you play the accompaniment and I'll go on home." I couldn't believe what I was saying. Get a grip, Annie, I thought. This is no big deal.

"I can't play and sing with those guys at the same time," Christina said easily, "and here they are. Finally."

"Let's get at it," Dan said. "We'll sing it three times, Annie, then we're outa here."

"Fine with me." I struck the pitch chord.

The four of them gathered around the piano and did a ragged run-through.

"I don't think it's fast enough," Christina said.

"It's a stupid song," Dan complained. "'A-dicka-dick. A-dicka-dick.' If I'd known I had to sing this junk, I wouldn't have auditioned at all."

"Yeah, we ought to quit," Eric said.

"It'll be over faster if we sing it faster," Christina said. "Like this, Annie." She leaned over my shoulder and fingered the melody expertly.

"All right." I twisted my shoulder from under her arm.

"Well, I've been listening to the record, so I know how it goes." Christina turned back to her suitors. "From the beginning, guys, and Randy, get the words right this time. The line's 'still spraying my decaying family tree.'"

"Yes, ma'am." Randy gave her an Elizabethan bow.

That was when I realized they liked her. Two weeks ago nobody had even noticed her, and now she was running a rehearsal. And they were enjoying it, too.

"Any time this century," she said at my shoulder, and I struck the first note.

During the next run-through, Ms. Dalton arrived to listen. "That's coming along," she said when we'd finished. "Annie, I'm sending Peter in here to go through the 'I've Come to Wive' number with these fellows. Can you play it for them?"

I thumbed through the score and flattened the book at the binding. "I'm not much for sight reading, but I'll try."

"I can do it, Ms. Dalton," Christina said. "I mean, I think I can play it a little bit."

"Then help yourself." I smiled at everybody, but my face felt pinched.

"As long as it gets done," Ms. Dalton said, smiling broadly as if Christina were a great discovery she'd just made.

"I'll see you at home," Christina called after me, but I didn't answer.

જ

Greg was in the kitchen when I came in. I flung my book bag on the table and went to the refrigerator to peer in under his arm.

"So who rattled your cage?" he asked, waiting for me to pick an apple from the crisper.

"Nobody."

"Don't give me that." He closed the door and put his hand on my shoulder for a moment before backing off. "Ouch," he said, like he'd been stung. "You're as mad as a hornet."

"Yeah well, I'll survive it."

"What's up, gang?" Dad asked from the doorway.

He closed his book on his finger, holding his place. "Having a little snack, huh? I'll take part of that." He pointed to the apple I was quartering.

"Annie's bent out of shape," Greg said, sliding past me to go upstairs.

"So?" Dad took the apple section I offered him.

"It's nothing, Dad. Just a bad day."

"Well, tell me about it. Let me commiserate a little, why don't you?" He sat down at the table and folded a napkin for a bookmark in his book.

"Christina brought up the Shakespeare question in English today." Saying it, I felt so silly. How petty could I get?

"So, what's the problem?"

"Oh, I don't know. I guess I just didn't want it mentioned. I mean, it wasn't hers, Dad. She didn't know anything about it till Tuesday and she has to bring it up in class. Then Ms. Langley wanted to know all about it. I don't know, I felt implicated or something."

"Well, that's probably the end of it," Dad said.

"Maybe." I cut into a wedge of cheese and handed him a slice. "Then I played for a rehearsal this afternoon and the music was hard and I was sight reading. Christina could play it better."

"So this is about Christina, huh?"

"I guess so." I gave him a sheepish smile. "I thought she was a poor little waif, and now—"

"You've rescued her and she's taking over the boat," he said.

"Yeah. And I guess I'm p.o.'d about it."

"Do you want to rescind your hospitality?"

"No, I can't do that! She's got the part and she's doing a great job. Ms. Dalton said so. I can't do anything now."

"Then I guess you'll have to make the best of it."

"I thought I'd like her. I mean, what's not to like?"

"Well, maybe this is just a bad day, like you said. Tomorrow you'll probably feel better about her."

"But what about this afternoon? She'll be here any minute."

He put his arms around me. "We both know you'll be nice to her, Annie. That's how you are."

"Thanks, Dad." I hugged him back, although that wasn't exactly what I wanted to hear. When I went upstairs, I was still dreading the doorbell's ring.

≈

I let Christina in and watched wordlessly while she hung her faded blue coat on the hall rack beside my own bright-red one.

"You're upset, aren't you?" she said, following me upstairs. "You're mad because I brought up the Shakespeare thing and I shouldn't have. I could tell you were mad. Then I took over the piano just like I didn't know that was wrong, too. Well, I shouldn't have done that either, Annie. You play just fine, you really do." She gave me a grave little smile and sat down on one of the twin beds. "This play means so much to me, Annie. You mean so much to me. I couldn't be doing anything if it weren't for you."

I flopped backward on the other bed and put my arm over my eyes. I had never heard her say this much at one time. Just listening seemed to take all my energy. Besides, I didn't want to see her looking beautiful and mournful at the same time. I'd had enough dramatics for one day. "You don't need to apologize," I said.

"But I don't want you to be mad at me, Annie. I couldn't stand it if you were." Her voice was muffled but I still didn't look.

"I'm not mad. I'm just tired." The moment I said it, I really did feel exhausted. I rolled over on my side to see Christina rummaging through her bag for a tissue.

"Here." I offered her the box from the bedside table. "You want something to eat?"

"No, I couldn't." She dabbed at her eyes and looked away.

"Oh come on. You're too skinny, you know. We'll find you a piece of cake."

"I can't," Christina said. She was truly crying now. "And stop being so nice." She blew into a tissue and wiped her face again. "On the way over here, I was so afraid. I thought you wouldn't let me in."

"Christina, that's ridiculous." What could I do but put my arm around her shoulder? "Of course I'd let you in."

Later that night on the phone, I said to Jill, "She was truly scared. How can you stay mad at somebody who's absolutely shaking in their shoes?"

"You can't." Jill sighed. "You have to be nice to her."

"But you still don't approve." I socked my pillow behind my neck, getting comfortable.

"It's not my place to approve," Jill said. "Anyway, I called with news of my own, not to listen to you moping around about Christina. Are you finished?"

"I guess so."

"Dan called me a little while ago. He wants me to go to the dance after the basketball game next Friday!"

"Wow! What did you say?"

"I was extremely cool. I said I'd let him know."

"You did not!" I laughed. "You said you'd go!"

"Well, it seemed like a good idea at the time." Jill paused. "Actually, I was so excited I could hardly talk. I did manage to say 'yes' though."

"Next Friday, right? Maybe Peter will ask me and we'll see you there."

"If he doesn't, you ask him. I want you there. I need you, Annie!"

I was remembering how Peter had said good night Saturday. He'd held my face in his hands and given me a lingering kiss as if he didn't want to let go. "He'll ask me," I said. "See you tomorrow."

"Yeah. Sweet dreams."

"Night." I hung up and switched off the light. The night-light in the hall splayed a feathery golden light on the wall. I lay there imagining the school cafeteria, the air still thick with cooking smells but the lights low and the music making the place suddenly magical. I could feel the warmth of Peter's arms around me, and I went to sleep without another thought about Christina.

7

I didn't want to admit to myself that I was still irritated with Christina on Monday. I had ignored her easily enough before Friday's English class, and since she never came to the cafeteria, I hadn't had to deal with her there. I had been relieved, too, not to have rehearsal that afternoon and then a free weekend. I remember feeling a slight curl of guilt creeping into the lightness I felt at the prospect of being at home without her. Maybe I wasn't as magnanimous as I pretended to be.

On Monday I didn't see her at rehearsal, so I assumed she'd gone home on the bus, but the minute I opened the front door that afternoon, I heard her in the kitchen. She was talking to Mom while the aroma of baking bread wafted through the house.

"Hm-m, something smells good." I dropped my

coat and book bag on a chair.

"It's banana bread," Christina said.

I ducked into the refrigerator. "Mom, is this all the milk?"

"Drink it. I'll send Greg on a milk run when he gets here. Christina suggested I put cinnamon and nutmeg in the bread, so I'm trying it," she said.

"My mom does," Christina said.

"Well, I wouldn't be messing with Grandma's recipe." I plopped the milk jug on the counter and reached for a glass.

"Just to see how we like it." Mom was peering over her glasses at me.

I cut a hunk off one end of a bread loaf although it wasn't cool yet and I knew she liked us to make thin, neat slices. "So why weren't you at rehearsal?" I asked Christina.

"I have a scratchy throat, so Ms. Dalton wanted me to rest today."

Before I could ask why she hadn't gone home on the bus, Mom took over. "It doesn't look serious," she said, "but I made her a hot lemonade."

"I feel a lot better already." Christina smiled and leaned back in her chair until its back rested against the wall. "We've been talking about Shakespeare."

"Really?"

"And about social life at school," Mom added. "Isn't there a dance next Friday? I was just telling Christina she should go."

"Anybody with an I.D. and two dollars can go." I set my glass in the sink and grabbed my coat and books. "I've got a French test tomorrow. See you later."

Upstairs in my room, I lay on my bed knowing I shouldn't have left Christina downstairs like that. The situation was my responsibility. That had been the deal. But Mom seemed so willing, as if she really enjoyed having Christina to talk to.

New energy, she'd called it when Greg's best friend in the eighth grade moved in with us for the last month of school so he could graduate with his class. His parents had come from their new home in Georgia for the ceremony and taken him away the next morning amid hugs and tears. "He's like one of our own," Mom had said, giving him one last hug before the embarrassed kid, tearful himself, could get settled among his belongings in the backseat of his family's station wagon. Now exchanging Christmas cards was our only contact, but I knew Mom still remembered him like a lost child, recalled with nostalgia the energy he'd created. And now here was Christina who seemed right at home.

The house was quiet, the sun already setting. My walls were shadowed, but I didn't turn on the light. From outside there came a shrieking cry, a bird's lonely wintry call. Could it be Rosie? No, Rosie was cozy in the mews, protected and safe. Peter saw to that. I reached for the phone to call him, then stopped myself, put my hand back across my chest and with a deep sigh, breathed in the scent of spicy bread from below. I had no reason to be angry.

I was still lying there when the phone rang. I reached for the receiver midway through the first ring.

It was Jill. "What are you doing?"

"Just lying here thinking."

"Sounds dangerous to me. About what?"

"You don't want to know."

"Christina." I heard an impatient sigh, then she went on. "I didn't see her all afternoon, so I thought maybe she'd disappeared—you know, vanished into thin air or something like that."

"She's here, letting Mom take care of her sore throat."

"Jeez. I thought her mother was a doctor or something."

"Nurse practitioner."

"Whatever. Listen, I'm calling about tomorrow

night. We're going to the basketball game, right?"

"Yeah. Peter's got the car so you can ride with us. Maybe Dan needs a ride, too. Why don't you ask him?"

"You've got to be kidding. I couldn't do that. He'd think I was chasing him."

"Well, you are, aren't you? Anyway, a thirty-minute ride to Huntsville and back is hardly a date."

"You do it," Jill pleaded. "Or get Peter to ask him. Please . . . please, please."

"Okay," I said wearily. "But just this once, Jill. The guy wouldn't have asked you to the dance if he didn't like you."

"You can say that. You know how Peter feels about you. You don't have all this agony."

I could hear Ms. Moore's car in the drive. The horn sounded, then the car door shut. "Got to go, Jill."

I sprinted downstairs in time to open the door before the bell rang. "Hi, Ms. Moore." I gave her what I hoped was a welcoming smile.

It was the only time she'd come to the door since that first afternoon, and I wanted a good look at her. I could see she'd probably been pretty once, but now, with her hair pulled back in a tight ponytail and her lipstick worn to a thin outline, she just looked tired. "Come on in."

"I really can't." She forced a smile in my direction but didn't cross the threshold. "I blew the horn."

"Christina's in the kitchen. She's not feeling well."

Just then Mom came into the foyer, Christina in tow. "Just a little sore throat," Mom said.

"You should have called me, Christina." Ms. Moore was frowning at all of us.

"I really don't think it's serious," Mom said.

"Maybe not, but I'll check her out. Let's get going, kid." Halfway across the porch, she turned back to us. "Thanks."

"See you tomorrow, Annie," Christina said.

"Sure. Tomorrow. Hope you feel better."

"I already do." She smiled, closing the door between us.

≥❧

"We've got to find Christina a date for the dance," I said to Peter and Jill the next day at lunch.

"What's this 'got to' stuff? I haven't got to do anything," Jill said.

"Well, let's do it anyway," I said easily. "Just so I

don't spend the evening thinking about her at home by herself."

"I'll buy that," Peter said. "I want your full attention."

"So your mom's putting a guilt trip on you," Jill said, crunching into her salad.

My patience was paying off. "Maybe a little. But the fact is Christina doesn't really know anybody and we do."

"I thought you were p.o.'d with her over the Shakespeare thing," Jill said. "Have you heard the latest, Peter? Ms. Langley is making us debate the authorship question in class, and if we don't participate, we have to write a boring old research paper on *Julius Caesar*. Ugh."

"And which are you doing?" Peter asked me.

"She didn't have any choice. Ms. Langley made her the head of the anti-Stratford group," Jill said, "and then Dan volunteered to lead the pro-Stratford group, so now what am I supposed to do? My best friend and an absolute hunk, and I have to choose."

"You're supposed to choose a position, Jill, not a personality," I said.

"Or a physique," Peter added.

"I know that! But I don't care who wrote the dumb old plays—I don't understand them anyway."

81

"We watched *Romeo and Juliet* on video last summer and you and Martha both cried," I reminded her. "You loved it."

"Well, that was the movie version," Jill said. "I made a C on the unit last year when we read it in class. A C! Mom had a fit!"

"What about *Hamlet?*" Peter asked. "You saw that."

"Just because Mel Gibson was in it," Jill said. "I'd go see Mel Gibson open soup cans."

Peter laughed. "So which team is Christina on, as if I couldn't guess."

"Actually, we don't know. We have until tomorrow to sign up. Meanwhile, help me think of somebody who would go to the dance with her."

"Oh, well." Jill sighed. "Make a list of dorks and we'll stick a pin in one."

"Jill!" I couldn't help laughing. "Seriously, what do you think about Randy Dail? He's in *Kiss Me, Kate*—they even do a song together."

"But he's such a sweetheart," Jill said. "I didn't know we were trying to think of somebody nice."

"Of course we are. Christina's okay, Jill. She really is. She's not that different from us. She just hasn't had a lot of advantages we've had." I sounded just like Mom.

"I don't know about that," Peter said. "I heard her talking at rehearsal one day about going to Europe with her high school chorus last year. I'm still waiting for a trip like that."

"I'm talking about here and now," I said. "Her social life is zilch and she doesn't have any friends but us. Come on, guys, help! Peter, will you please just ask Randy? I really think he likes her, and he's not dating anybody. They could hang out with us at the dance. It'll be fun."

Peter and Jill frowned at each other before Peter shrugged. "I'm not much for matchmaking," he said, "but I'll see how it goes."

"Great!" I could finally start eating lunch.

"But what about me?" Jill wanted to know. "Did you offer Dan a ride to the game tonight?"

"I did," Peter said.

"And?"

"He wanted to know who else was going."

"And what did you say?" Jill was practically bouncing off her seat.

"I said Annie—and you." Peter was grinning.

"Peter, tell me!"

"He said okay."

Jill looked dejected. "Just 'okay'? That's all he said?"

"Actually, he said he was planning to watch wrestling on TV but . . ."

"He did not!"

"Yes, he did. But he'd go to the game—since you're going."

"See, I told you," I said.

"Oh God, I can't believe it. He's choosing me over wrestling." Jill shook her sweater away from her chest. "Oh, I'm so hot. Don't you think it's hot in here?"

"Not especially, but you sure look flushed," I said.

Jill ignored me. "Now what am I going to do about the debate teams? Which one do I join?"

"The right one," Peter said.

"No, the left one," I said.

"Oh, you guys, I don't even know what you're talking about. There's no right and left to it," Jill complained.

"Sure there is," Peter said. "The conservative view is the right, the liberal view is the left."

"But which is which?" Jill groaned.

"I think you ought to write the research paper." I laughed. "And avoid polarizing altogether."

"No way. I've just decided," Jill said. "I'm on your team."

"But what about Dan?" Peter asked.

"Hey, being on opposite sides could mean the beginning of a great romance."

"Like *Romeo and Juliet*." I teased her.

"Poor Dan," Peter said. "I think he's going to find out more about women than he'll ever know about Shakespeare."

"And he's going to enjoy it, too. Wait and see." Jill got up. "I'm going to sign up right now."

We watched her slide her tray onto the conveyor belt.

"You're going to have excellent help," Peter said sympathetically.

"Yeah. A project I don't want and help I don't need. It's working out great."

"You want to fly Rosie Saturday? Afterward we could get something to eat, go to a movie."

"Sure." But I wasn't very enthusiastic.

"Don't worry so much. We'll get Christina a date, and the Shakespeare business will be over before you know it. The play, too. Everything will be back to normal by spring."

I gave him my best smile. "I know," I said. "I'm not one bit worried."

8

"Well, it's not the end of the world," Mom said the next night at dinner when I told my family about Ms. Langley's plans for the debate. "In fact, I think it's a great idea. I'll help you. We'll all help."

"Don't look at me," Greg said. "It's not my fight. Not anymore, it's not."

"And I don't even know anything about Shakespeare except what you tell me," Martha complained. "I don't see how I can help."

"Then I guess you mean me," Dad said. "Give me an excuse, kids."

"You don't have one!" Mom said firmly. "Annie, why don't you have your committee come over Monday night? Larry, would you check at the university library for us in case they have some new research on the subject? I doubt they do. It's just amazing how hidden this information is—English majors graduating without ever hearing there's even a controversy."

"There she blows!" Dad called, making Mom blush.

"Anyway, I imagine we'll have to rely on my meager little shelf of resources," she went on, trying to stay calm. "Heavens, it's so much fun to *educate*—I can't help but be excited about this."

"That's great for you, Mom, but what about Ms. Langley? Shouldn't somebody tell her about Mr. Johnson? He's the head of English, you know, and he's got a very short fuse," Greg said. "Jeez, this thing's got trouble written all over it."

"Well, there's no such thing as academic freedom in public schools, not like there's supposed to be in colleges, but I imagine Ms. Langley can do anything she wants in class as long as she keeps within the curriculum guidelines," Dad said. "She's supposed to be teaching a unit on Shakespeare, isn't she?"

"Julius Caesar." I was glum.

"Well, you seem less than excited," Mom said.

I knew how she was going to love it. I knew she'd take over, too, not that I cared. Let her do it, I thought. She can call all the meetings she wants to. "I have to admit the class seemed interested," I said.

"Everybody loves a whodunit," Greg said.

"But we know who did it. The Seventeenth Earl of Oxford," Martha announced.

"He's definitely the best candidate," Mom said, ignoring my frown. "And if a fraction of the time and effort, not to mention the money, exerted on William Shakespeare of Stratford were spent investigating Edward de Vere, we'd be getting somewhere."

"I still think Ms. Langley's in for it. She's young, she's new, she's got the kind of enthusiasm that makes old Johnson squirm," Greg said.

"But she's got a class of kids who are awake," Mom countered. "That ought to count for something."

❧

Saturday afternoon was cold with wind that blew the clouds into tatters and swept under my jacket as if determined to obliterate the warmth I'd trapped between layers of clothing.

"I know you don't like to hunt," Peter had said when I'd climbed into the Jeep, Rosie hooded on her perch between us. "But Dad didn't get her out but once this week, and she needs a kill for her self-respect. Besides, the freezer's almost empty."

"Whatever." For once I didn't even try to hide my bad mood.

"What's going on?" Peter asked after a mile of silence.

"Nothing. Everything's just great." I really didn't want to punish Peter when none of my problems were his fault. Anyway, they weren't really problems. Problems were starvation and people living in cars, drive-by shootings, AIDS. The troubles at 248 Reynolds Drive were nothing at all.

"Come on, Annie. You look like somebody died," Peter said.

"Well, they didn't." Wasn't I the one always ready to be helpful, to supply an answer, to make a joke? I didn't know how to let him comfort me. "Just a fight with Mom. Well, not really a fight, just—"

"I know," Peter said. "Our house isn't exactly fracas free."

"Well, mine used to be. Now I don't know. I just want her to leave me alone."

"Hey, name three—no, name one girl who gets along with her mother and I'll show you a weirdo. My sisters either sulked or cried for years. Now Beth's married and Karen's in college, and they both think Mom's the greatest."

I could feel myself breaking. "She's all excited about this Shakespeare thing. You know she's always got to have a project, like being the Arts Council director and all the other stuff she does isn't enough. So now she's all into this debate when I didn't want to get involved in the first place. I'm so busy at school now I can't think straight. I got eighty-four on a French test last week. Mom says if I'd just get organized—well, I am organized but I'm not a machine like she is. I can't do everything perfectly. The day after my French test, I came down before dinner to set the table and Christina had already done it. She'd even made a centerpiece out of some bittersweet and dried stuff Mom had. Everybody went on and on about it like she was brilliant or something." I blew my nose, and Rosie cocked her head to the new sound. "I'm being ridiculous."

"But it's how you feel," Peter said.

"One thing for sure, I'll never drive with Mom again. This morning we were going downtown, so I said I'd drive. I need to practice, you know. But then she yelled at me the whole time, when she wasn't putting her foot through the floorboard. I was so furious, I just refused to drive home. What am I going to do? It'll be May and I won't have practiced at all."

"Nobody should have to drive with their mother." Peter stopped the Jeep beside a field that bordered a deep woods. "Look, Annie, if you need to go somewhere and just talk——"

"It's okay." I forced a little smile and tried to lighten my voice.

"We won't be long," Peter said.

But off the fist, Rosie found a perch on a high pine limb. I stayed near the Jeep while Peter walked into the field, the dry winter brush crushing under his boots. I leaned against the fender waiting. I wouldn't have come if I'd known that Rosie was going to hunt, and yet I couldn't help watching, at least from a distance.

"This is how the natural world works," Peter had often told me. "Just remember, she's wild. All her instincts tell her to hunt, even tell her how."

Suddenly I could hear Rosie's bell, and I looked up to watch her quick strokes off the perch, then a rushing swoop groundward. She pulled up fast, talons empty, but this time instead of returning to her perch, she rose in the sky, flapping two or three times onto a thermal, where she hung, watching. Now she knew there were rabbits.

Peter was striding toward me, stirring the grass as he walked. Above us, Rosie waited. Suddenly there was a scurrying beyond Peter, a rabbit fleeing toward the woods. The hawk hung another second, then folded and plummeted down, clutching the terrified rabbit like a cushion she'd come to rest on. I turned away as she curved her wings around the prey. I knew Peter intended to let her feed awhile, so I stayed at the Jeep, watching dusk streak the sky with shades of mauve.

I was getting cold, but there was another feeling, too, a sadness stirring in my chest as if Peter and the bird were completely separate from me. I felt invisible. Then a memory seeped into the loneliness and I let myself go with it, pushed backward in time. Where had I felt this way before?

At summer camp when I was nine. My first camp, my first week away from home. The wooded cabins had smelled funny, like a cellar, and at night the bunk had felt damp. My flowered sheets, my stuffed polar bear, the smell from a little canister of Mom's bath powder she'd let me bring along—none of them gave me comfort. Nothing would do but home itself, I told myself during that first night of wide-eyed terror while the girls around me slept. Tomorrow I would go home.

But the next morning, the schedule of activities put me on a roller coaster of busyness I couldn't jump off of, and that night I slept exhausted, my arms and legs numb from rowing and swimming and archery, my stomach stuffed with hearty food, my head bursting with names and camp songs and regulations that seemed like the happy directions to a new life.

Well, I'm definitely not homesick now, I thought. Peter had Rosie on his fist and was bringing her in. Maybe I'm sick of home.

"God, for a second back there, I thought she wasn't coming in," Peter said, settling the bird on the perch in the Jeep. "It was the strangest feeling, knowing there was nothing I could do, not a thing. Someday it's going to happen, too."

"I didn't think red-tails were that adventurous. Your dad told me about one he set free that kept coming back. He couldn't get rid of her." Why was I still so irritable?

"It happens, but it won't be that way with Rosie." He dropped his equipment on the backseat. "Want to get a pizza after I put her in?"

"I guess." I shut the door hard.

"Or there's a party at Amanda's we can go to," he said.

"No thanks." What did I expect from him, anyway?

"Maybe a party's what you need." Peter turned the Jeep onto the highway.

"No, I'd rather be alone with you." I wanted to make us both feel better.

"Then maybe you could try acting like it," he said, watching the road.

9

"Randy said he'd call her," Peter said in the band room after Monday's rehearsal, "but I don't know. He was surprised. I had to tell him she'll say yes if he calls. She will, won't she?"

"I'm sure she will," I said.

"Don't count on it. I think she's too weird to be predictable." Jill shrugged. "I don't see what you're bothering for, anyway, because the guy she's really interested in is a lot closer to home."

"Who?" Peter asked.

"Why, Greg, of course. Haven't you noticed how she looks at him? And when he's not around, she's always asking stuff about him."

"She does not." Sometimes Jill was the weird one. "Her own brother died. That's all it is."

"Well, I don't think she wants Greg for a

brother, that's for sure." Jill wasn't backing down this time. "When we have rehearsal breaks, she hangs around the gym. Now why is that?"

"It's where the water fountains and the rest rooms are," I countered. "Come on, Jill, give it up."

"She wants to spend Tuesday nights with you, doesn't she, so she can go to the game when she obviously wasn't interested in basketball before. We had to explain everything to her."

"You go to the games and you don't like sports," Peter reminded her.

"I know, and I admit it, too. I'm honest." Jill collected her belongings, then turned to me. "Are you going to the game tomorrow night?"

"I guess so. Do you think Mom and Dad would miss one?"

"You could, though. We could study. Gosh, I'm behind in everything!"

"You mean you don't want to look for Drew again?" I laughed.

"I certainly do not. Come home with me, okay? I'll rent a movie."

"I can't. Christina's staying over and going to Lawrence with us," I admitted.

"But I thought she was staying over tonight for the Shakespeare meeting," Jill said. She was standing

her ground, her arms akimbo and a frown wrin-
kling her forehead.

"She is."

"That's two nights in a row, Annie." She nudged
Peter. "Does this look like an invasion to you or
what?"

"I'm staying out of it." Peter slung his book bag
over his shoulder. "Behold, the fair Bianca!"

"Ready?" Christina asked, coming up behind us.
She moved ahead to push open the door. "Let's go
home. I'm starving!"

❧

"Randy Dail wants to ask you to go to the
dance on Friday," I said to Christina while we were
clearing the kitchen table for the meeting later that
evening.

"How do you know?" she asked, folding the
mats into their place in a drawer.

"He told Peter and Peter told me. That's how
things work. Everybody knows what everybody's
doing or thinking about doing or wanting to do
before anything happens," I said as lightly as I
could.

"I don't know," Christina said. "He's not really
my type."

I had to struggle not to show surprise. "Why, I

think he's cute, and he's funny and smart. What more do you want?"

"I guess I can tell you." Christina sat down at the table and gave me a grave little smile. "I had a boyfriend in Charlotte. We were really in love and then, well, Daddy found out about him. I thought I was going to be grounded forever and for no good reason. Jason was wonderful. He made good grades and was so handsome and nice, too, really nice. Absolutely the only thing Daddy could find wrong with him was that he was older than me."

"How much older?"

"A senior. He goes to N.C. State now."

"He was a senior when you were in ninth grade?"

"Uh-huh." Christina sighed. "Anyway, when Daddy found out, he wouldn't let me see him anymore. Jason had the neatest little red Datsun. Daddy absolutely hated that—my going out with him, you know, just the two of us alone on dates. That's one reason he agreed for Mom and me to move here. He didn't want Jason coming home on weekends to see me and all that."

I didn't know what to say. I was beginning to wonder if I was the only one who'd seen Christina as a sad little waif.

"Oh, Annie, I miss him so much," she went on softly. Her voice was trembling on every word. "Sometimes even now I can feel his arms around me. I can feel him kissing me." She looked up, her eyes misty and mouth quivering.

"Christina, I'm sorry," I started, then stopped, appalled by the tiny thought that had leaped into my head even as I was intent on sympathy. I wasn't absolutely sure I believed her.

❧

By quarter past seven, the six members of the anti-Stratford group were gathered around our kitchen table. Mom had insisted she join us for this initial meeting and I'd agreed. The more work she did, the less I'd have to do.

"After this session, you're staying out of it, right?" Dad had said at dinner. "Checking the card catalog at the library is one thing, but commanding the forces is another."

"I know, I know," Mom had said. She was irritated that he was putting a damper on her excitement. "But I do feel a little responsibility for this."

"Right, Mom," Martha said. "If you weren't a fruitcake, we wouldn't be nuts."

"I mean it, El." Dad was giving her a stern look.

"Oh, come off it, Larry. Who helped Martha

with her science project last year? She—excuse me, they—made a suspension bridge out of balsa wood and string," she said to Christina.

"I made it!" Martha said. "Daddy just watched!"

"And cut and glued a piece here and there," Mom said.

"Well, it was a big project," Dad said.

"And so is this. I tell you what, Larry, I'll help just the way you help in the kitchen," Mom said. "He always leaves one thing undone, Christina, like water in the sink or leftovers on the counter instead of putting them in the fridge, just to remind me it's not really his responsibility."

"I do not!" Dad grinned. "Well, sometimes I guess I do. But that doesn't relate in any way to your helping these kids."

"I know," Mom said, "but I had you going for a minute."

We laughed, even Christina, who had shrunk in her chair as if she'd expected to be caught between blows.

Now Dad was watching the news and Mom was at the table with us, Christina at her elbow.

"Ms. Langley gave us the rules for the debate today," I said. "She says it wouldn't be like we were on a real forensics team, because there's not that much time to get ready. What we've got is the proposition that says 'Resolved: That William Shakespeare of Stratford is the author of the poems and plays attributed to him.' The other team has the burden of proof, so their opening speech will probably be all the reasons people think the Stratford man is Shakespeare. Then we give our speech refuting them. After that, we have these little arguments based on the opening speech and rebuttal, so everybody gets time to speak."

"Not me," Ernie said. "I just signed up so I don't have to write a dumb paper."

"It says right here everybody has to say something." Jill pointed to the guidelines. "Or you don't get a grade."

"Aw, man." Ernie shook his head in disgust.

Eric laughed. "Them's the breaks, Ern."

"Ms. Gerhardt knows a lot about this," Christina said. "Maybe she could tell us how to get started."

Jill rolled her eyes at me, but I avoided her by turning to Mom. "Okay, Mom. Any suggestions?"

"Well, here's a list of books on the authorship question in the university library. I was pleased to see there are several supporting the anti-Stratford view. I think somebody should get a couple of them tomorrow, since I don't think there's anything on the subject in your school library."

"I checked today, and there's nothing," Christina said.

"Don't we need to know what they're going to say so we can base our opening speech on that?" Phoebe asked. Always organized, she had her pencil poised on a clean legal pad.

"No telling what Dan will come up with," Jill said. "Of course, Friday night I could try to find out."

"I think we'd better have more reliable research than that," Christina said.

"Well, lah-de-dah." Jill shrugged. "It was a joke, Christina. A joke."

Phoebe said, "We should decide who's going to do what. For example, who's going to make our opening statement?"

"I think Annie should," Christina said. "She's our leader."

"I agree," Jill said.

"Fine by me," Ernie said. "I don't want to say nothing at all."

"Ms. Langley said we could have class time tomorrow to work on it," Eric said.

"Maybe you could take Annie and me to the

university library tonight," Christina said to Mom. "So we'll be ready tomorrow."

"Sure," Mom said, "and I have something to give you now. I think the other team has an advantage because your textbook gives the Stratfordian perspective." She handed out copies of a page from a book. "It's a list of reasons the William Shaksper—we'll call him that—who was known to be from Stratford is not a likely candidate for authorship. Just take it home and study it. You see, all you have to do to win is cast doubt on the Stratford man. You don't have to prove who actually wrote the plays. Who's going to be your audience, anyway? Not just the people who opted to write boring papers, I hope."

"Ms. Langley said she was going to try to get the other English classes that meet that hour to be there," Jill said. "I, for one, hope nobody comes."

"I hope everybody does," Christina said. "I'm so excited!"

"Good!" Mom actually put her arm around her. "I'm always glad to make a convert."

❧

"Randy called and Christina said 'yes,'" I whispered into the phone at bedtime.

"Great," Jill said. "Now we can all rest easy tonight."

I ignored her sarcasm. "So we'll go together," I whispered. "And you be nice to her, Jill. I mean it."

"Why are you whispering?" Jill wanted to know.

"She's next door in Martha's room."

"Yeah, well, she's always somewhere," Jill said. "Remember how we used to talk every night?"

"I remember the time you fell asleep with the phone at your ear and the recording said 'Please hang up the phone' for hours."

"I was dead to the world." Jill laughed. "For years I've said good night to you last, Annie."

"I know." I forced myself to use my normal voice. "Me too."

"And now there's Christina."

"Yeah, well, here she is," I whispered.

"Night, Annie."

"Okay."

Christina was in the other bed and I'd turned out the light before I realized I'd hung up without really telling Jill good night.

10

I watched from the wings while the cast rehearsed Petruchio and Katharine's scene in Petruchio's house.

"Now remember," Ms. Dalton called from the aisle, "this is the first scene after a very unhappy wedding. You've been traveling a long time, Kate, and you're tired and dirty and look a mess. You don't look so good yourself, Petruchio, but you're on home ground. You've got the advantage now, and you're determined to break her."

"Yeah, Peter." Eric was playing one of the servants. "Think of her as a horse."

"Cute," Amanda said, pulling back from them and taking a haughty stance. Her red hair shimmered under the lights. "Really cute."

"Let's do it, then!" Ms. Dalton barked. "From

your line 'Food! Food!' Peter, really roar."

Peter pulled the cushion from under Amanda while speaking a line to Eric, then grabbed a fake beef joint just as she was getting it to her mouth.

"His timing's great," Christina whispered at my shoulder. I hadn't heard her slip in. "Ms. Langley's hunting for you," she went on. "I just passed her in the breezeway, and she looked extremely grim."

Onstage Kate was saying, "Did you marry me to famish me?"

"I'm famished myself," Christina whispered. "Do you have any money? I'll pay you back."

I pushed my hand deep into the pocket of my jeans. "Here." Change dropped into Christina's hand.

"Until tomorrow," Christina said, cupping the money.

"Whenever." I headed out through the wings toward the main classroom building, my mind already sprinting ahead. Why was Ms. Langley at school this late and what could she want with me?

"There you are." She settled her briefcase on the walk, then slipped into her coat and sat down on the low wall that enclosed the breezeway. She held her collar closed at her throat. "We've run into a problem with the debate, Annie. I intend to tell the class tomorrow, but I thought since you were still here, I'd give you some warning."

"Mr. Johnson?" I sat down next to her. A cold wind was whipping under the awning. I pulled my jacket tighter, too.

"I'm afraid so." Ms. Langley frowned out toward the practice field beyond the gym. "In our department meeting just now, I invited the other fourth-period English classes to serve as audience and judges for the debate. Mr. Johnson wanted to know the subject matter, and when I told him— well, I won't go into details but let's say he voiced strong objections."

"He's opposed to everything," I said.

"No." Ms. Langley shook her head. "I'm sure he's a fine teacher, and in the three years I've been here, I haven't found him unreasonable. Of course, this is the first real ripple I've made in the waters." She smiled a little and looked at me. "I'll have to admit he went a bit overboard about this, but what can I do? I'm not tenured yet."

"You mean if we go ahead with the debate, you could lose your job?" It seemed like such a ridiculous question, because she was a great teacher.

"Oh, probably not. But he told me in no uncertain terms to call the whole thing off, and I don't see that I have much choice but to do that." She stood up, looked out at the sky again, then wearily lifted her briefcase. "I'm sorry, Annie. Actually, the thing I'm most sorry about is that the class seemed so excited about this issue and it's been reflected in their interest in the play."

"Yeah. Even Ernie's showing signs of life." I didn't want to make her feel worse, but I did want her to know what she was giving up. "Today he stopped me in the hall to show me an article he'd found. I didn't think he even knew we had a library."

"Oh well." Ms. Langley sighed, hugging herself against the cold. "You'd better go back to rehearsal. I'll talk to the class tomorrow. Maybe by then I'll have come up with another project that will spark as much interest."

"Sure," I said without much enthusiasm. "See you." I headed back to the theater but then stopped at the entrance to watch her walking across the parking lot to her car. I knew being reprimanded in the faculty meeting must have been painful for her, but she was doing a great job of covering it up.

"Ms. Langley, I'm not sure it's over yet!" I was surprised at how determined I sounded.

She didn't turn around. The wind had taken my words the other way.

"I've been thinking about Christina and the dance tomorrow night. Maybe you should lend her something of yours?" Mom said after Ms. Moore's horn had sounded impatiently and Christina had disappeared into the night. "Her clothes are so— well, sad-looking."

When I didn't respond, Mom went on, "Why don't you call and offer her something—how about that vest we gave you for Christmas? You don't ever wear it."

We were on the sofa waiting for Dad to come home for dinner, and the fire I'd made brightened the room against the cold darkness pressing in from the windows. I pushed myself deeper into the cushions and hugged a pillow to my chest.

"I was saving it." I kept staring at the fire. I wanted to tell her to stay out of my business—and my closet—but I didn't, although lately, she seemed to have something to say about everything, whether I wanted her opinion or not.

"Oh." She sipped her wine. "I thought you didn't like it—which is perfectly all right, of course. I shouldn't be trying to buy you clothes anyway. Everybody is so hard to fit. So particular, too."

"I like the vest, Mom. I love it. I was planning to wear it to the dance myself."

She didn't seem to notice my irritation at all. "Well, could you offer her something else then? Maybe if she has something nice to wear, she'll feel more comfortable."

"I think she feels fine," I said.

"I don't know." Her voice went suddenly soft, as if she were talking about something really precious. "There's an awkwardness about her that really tugs at me."

"I'll think of something and call her later." I pushed myself up and switched on a lamp. The light spilled across Mom's face, and her expression, so open with thoughtfulness, made me turn away. I looked into the blaze instead, not wanting to see her concern for Christina so blatantly exposed. My stomach flipped and I wondered for a moment if this was what jealousy felt like. There was something dark and slippery in my gut.

"The Shakespeare debate bit the dust today." I knew that would shatter the restful quiet she'd been enjoying.

"Why?" She uncurled on the sofa and put her glass on the end table.

"Mr. Johnson told Ms. Langley we couldn't do

it." I had her attention now. The cool coil in my stomach dissolved.

"But he can't do that!"

"Yes, he can," Greg called from the kitchen. He came in, peeling off his sweat jacket. "Gosh, it's cold. The wind chill factor must be ten below."

"And Larry's not home yet." Now Mom was fretful about everything.

"He pulled up just as I was coming in," Greg said. He stopped by the sofa and brushed his hand against her cheek.

She winced and drew away. "Goodness, honey, weren't you wearing gloves?"

"Can't find them," Greg said. He stretched his hands out behind him and leaned backward toward the fire. "So the debate is off?"

"As far as Mr. Johnson's concerned, it is," I said. "Of course, we knew all along this could happen, and I thought I wouldn't care. I mean, I don't have time for it anyway. But now that it's called off— now that somebody's saying we can't do it—I sort of want to hang in there." I sat down on the sofa arm near Mom.

"Hang in how?" Greg asked.

"I don't know exactly. Take it to the principal, the school board. Do something." I felt the warm strength of Mom's hand on my thigh. It would have been easy enough to pull away, but I didn't.

"Alice Fletcher is a reasonable person," she said. "Maybe you should talk to her."

"Yeah sure, she's okay," Greg said, "but she's still the principal. I, for one, never go near the principal's office. No matter what."

"I'm not surprised. They could have a warrant for your arrest in there," Dad said from the doorway.

"They probably do. Failure to hand in homework for six consecutive weeks," I said. "Dad, did you hear? The debate is off."

"Temporarily." Mom patted my leg. "Our daughter is contemplating assertive action. You could write a letter to the student newspaper," she said to me. "You could get a petition going expressing your belief in open inquiry. You could—"

"Eat dinner," Dad said. "I skipped lunch."

Mom got up reluctantly. "Here we've got all this powerful food for thought and you're thinking about your stomach."

"Every time I feed the body, I'm also feeding the mind, not to mention the soul," Dad said, putting one arm around her. "Call Martha, Greg, while we get this show on the road." He opened his other arm to me. "So the battle begins." He held me close to his side for a moment. "Is that what you want?"

"I don't know, Dad. I just feel like I should do something."

"You know, you two are just alike," he said, drawing Mom and me into the kitchen.

No, we're not. I don't want to be like her, I thought. But I couldn't say it. Maybe he was right, anyway.

ॐ

Later that night, after I'd talked to Peter and Jill, I called Christina. "I was just deciding what to wear tomorrow night," I said as casually as I could. "You know, to the game and the dance. I'll probably wear that vest I got for Christmas. Anyway, I thought you could borrow my red sweater. I know it'll look great with your dark hair, and I'm not planning to wear it."

There was silence. "Christina, are you there?"

"I couldn't. Everybody would know it's yours."

"No, they wouldn't. Nobody thinks about things like that."

"Jill does."

"Well, she wouldn't say anything." I could hear the growing irritation in my voice. Here I was, offering her the clothes off my back and she wasn't even grateful. So much for forced generosity. "Anyway, you can wear it if you want to."

"I have something," Christina said softly. "Dad sent me money this week, and tonight Mom took me all the way back to the mall to buy a sweater."

"Hey, that's great!" I frowned at the phone, wishing I'd followed my own instincts and ignored Mom. Why did I let her get me into predicaments like this? "I'll see you tomorrow then."

"Okay. Good night, Annie." Christina's voice faded, then came back strong. "I guess I should thank you for offering."

"Yeah, well, good night." I hung up and flopped back on the bed. I considered finding Mom and telling her what had happened, but what good would it do? She'd still think it was right to offer.

I wished I hadn't already talked to Peter. I couldn't call him again because he didn't have a phone in the attic and I'd have to disturb his parents. I hadn't even told him about Mr. Johnson and the debate. Maybe he'd think I should drop it like Greg did. Guys could do that. They could make a decision and then stop thinking about it. Well, I couldn't. But I'm not like Mom, I thought wearily. I don't want a cause a minute, not even a righteous one. I don't want to be like that.

I turned out the light and tried to get settled

under the covers. Even when I forced myself to be still, my mind kept racing, imagining a confrontation with Mr. Johnson, a meeting with the principal, the heady excitement of composing a letter to the newspaper, writing a petition statement. Stop it. I flopped onto my side, my arm pressed against my heart. Calm down.

I flipped through the images in my head, hunting for a comforting one, but instead I kept turning up a picture of Mom, her face pensive in the firelight. What did she want from me anyway? Perfection—that was it. Well, she wouldn't get it. Not in a million years.

Finally my mind rested on Peter at rehearsal that afternoon. Even in civvies he commanded the stage, became Petruchio. Someday he would probably play Shakespeare, *Hamlet* even. Someday. My mind spun away again, then caught on lyrics I'd been hearing for days. "Where is the life that late I led?" I heard in my head. "Where is it now? Totally dead. Where is the fun I used to find?" I fell asleep to the sound of Peter's singing.

11

"So the debate is off." I was in the cafeteria line with Peter.

Jill leaned back from her place in front of us. "Unless we do something. Annie was working on a letter to the paper even before Ms. Langley told the rest of the class."

"We could talk to Ms. Fletcher, too." The thin gray hamburger patties in the hot tray were as disgusting as usual, but I took one anyway. "God, I'll be glad when I'm a senior. Open lunch has got to be heaven."

"And give up all this?" Peter was selecting a burger for himself. "So you're going to talk to Ms. Fletcher?"

"What do you think? Is it worth it?"

We followed Jill to our table. "Dan and Phoebe

are eating with us, so we can discuss strategy," she said, dropping her book bag on the chair next to her. "Dan will sit here."

"Right, Jill, that's really important strategy." Peter laughed. We took seats on the other side. "If I did anything, I'd go to Ms. Fletcher first, because there's definitely no point in trying to meet with Johnson. Does Ms. Langley know what's going on?"

"No, there's really no time, because if we do anything at all, we have to get the letter written this afternoon for next Tuesday's paper. The following week's edition will be too late. Anyway, I think we should get an appointment with Ms. Fletcher before I talk to Ms. Langley."

"That way she can't stop us," Jill said, jumping up. "Here, Dan!" She cleared his place.

Dan and Phoebe brought their trays to the table. "So what's the plan?" Phoebe asked, taking the chair on the end.

"So far, a letter to the paper. You're on the staff, aren't you, Phoebe? If I get the letter to you later today, can you get it in?"

"No problem. It's probably the only controversy we've got."

"Okay. The letter and an appointment with Ms. Fletcher for the first of next week," I said.

"Then maybe a petition."

"Isn't that enough?" Dan wanted to know. "With rehearsal three afternoons, who's got time for an all-out war?"

"None of us," Jill agreed.

"But this is important," Phoebe said. As stage manager of the musical, she was as busy as the rest of us, but she loved a cause. "I've dealt with Ms. Fletcher several times. She supported the recycling program we started last year, and this year, she agreed to sell health-food snacks and juice at the concession stand. She let us publish that article about contraceptives, too. She's okay."

"But messing with Shakespeare is another thing altogether," Peter said. "I think you can expect her to stay out of this since it's a classroom issue. Internal affairs and all that."

"That's why our presentation to her can't be about Shakespeare. The issue has to be intellectual freedom," I reminded them.

"Wow, this sounds like big-time stuff," Dan said. "Do you guys really think we should be doing this? I mean, we could get in deep shit—pardon my French." He leaned back in his chair, waiting.

"I think we should," Phoebe said solemnly.

"Me too," Jill said. "I thought the whole thing

was a bore to begin with but"—she grinned at me—"now I'm convinced. We can't back down. I mean, they can't tell us we can't learn something, can they?"

"Hi." Christina was at her shoulder.

"Good grief, Christina, don't sneak up on people like that," Jill said.

"Sit." Peter pulled up a chair from another table for her. "Aren't you eating?"

"Not that plastic," Christina said. "I wanted to hear the plan, though. There still is one, isn't there?"

"We'll do the letter and talk to Ms. Fletcher," Phoebe said to get us back on track.

"What about Ms. Langley's mentor? Didn't Ms. Martinez observe our class once at the beginning of the year? Maybe she's the mentor," I said.

"Yuk, a science teacher," Jill said.

"But that could be a good thing," Phoebe said. "A scientist is interested in investigating, right?"

"Right," Peter said, getting up. "Well, I'll leave you subversives to it. Happy plotting." He leaned over, brushing his cheek against mine. "I'll see you tonight."

"See you." But the dance was the furthest thing from my mind.

"Hey, that's pretty!"

Christina was standing in the middle of my room wearing a new teal-blue turtleneck sweater. I ran my hand along the thick ribs of the sleeve. "Your dad must have sent you a bundle."

"Not really. It was on sale at Broydan's." She twirled around, letting me admire her. The shy girl in a tattered old sweater didn't seem to exist anymore.

"Well, it's beautiful. Perfect with your eyes." I studied her a moment. "Why, Christina, you're wearing makeup. I've never seen you in makeup before."

"I haven't worn any since we came here. My grandparents don't approve, so it's too big a hassle at home."

"What a drag." I slipped into my vest.

"That's why I brought some makeup here," Christina went on. "It's in Martha's room. She said I could keep it there."

"Sure, but you can keep it in here if you want. We'll find a place." I contemplated my cluttered dresser.

"Martha's room is fine. She has an empty drawer where I can put things." Christina sat down on the bed while I finished getting dressed. "Greg's coming to the dance, isn't he? I mean, everybody comes, don't they?"

"I guess so. I think he said he and Amanda would see us there. Looks like she's actually wearing him down."

Christina flopped backward on the bed. "I can't stand her," she said. "She's such a prima donna at rehearsals, it's sickening."

"Well, she does have the lead, you know."

"Barely. My part is almost as big as hers."

"What did you do, count lines?" I was surprised to be defending Amanda. Well, I'd known her for years and I'd never seen her really act the diva.

"She's a slut," Christina said. "A real sleaze."

"Who is?" Martha asked from the doorway.

"Nobody," I said.

"Amanda Pickens. She's all over Peter at rehearsals." Christina didn't seem to see from my expression that I wanted her to shut up. "If he were my boyfriend, I wouldn't put up with it," she went on.

"Christina, Amanda's had the hots for Greg for years, since grade school!" I said. "Martha, get out of here."

"I never get to hear anything interesting,"

Martha complained. "I'm not a baby, you know. I know about sluts."

"Scram, Martha!" I turned back to Christina, ready to tell her to watch what she said in front of Martha, but she had stretched out on the bed, her eyes closed.

"Hey," I said, but she didn't move. I went closer to peer down at the face, saw eye shadow perfectly applied in soft shades of gray, lashes blackened to fluffy wisps on her cheeks, rose blush lightly coloring the ridge of her cheekbones. "Hey, Christina, get up."

"Gotcha!" She lurched up, grabbing at me, and I tumbled onto the bed, twisting and rolling to avoid landing squarely on top of her.

I stayed there trying to catch my breath while Christina lay beside me, as still as stone. After a minute, she slid off the bed and stood in front of the mirror.

"Now I'll have to do my hair again," she said, pushing her fingers through the thick curls. "If it weren't so much trouble, I'd put it in a French braid." She leaned forward, studying herself for a moment. "Maybe Mom has time to do it."

She was out of the room on her way downstairs before I realized she meant my mother.

Even with the tables and chairs stored, the cafeteria was crowded. Peter held my hand while we maneuvered among the dancers to the other side of the room, where Jill and Dan were leaning against an opened window. Randy was with them.

"Where's Christina?" I asked.

"We haven't seen her since we got here," Jill said.

Randy shrugged, looking embarrassed. "She said she was going to the bathroom."

"And sometimes that takes hours," Peter said.

"Maybe you should go look for her," Jill suggested and Randy, looking relieved he'd been told what to do, wandered off around the edge of the dance floor.

"I feel like a jerk, setting him up with the invisible date," Peter said. "I knew it was a bad idea."

"So blame me." I dropped his hand. "Anyway, there she is." I pointed into the crowd of dancers who were barely moving in the tight quarters.

"Oh, my God, she's dancing with Greg!" Jill said.

"Amanda must be dead somewhere, because she'd never in a million years let this happen," Peter said.

"Maybe she's the one in the women's room," I said.

"Yeah, locked in a stall," Jill added. "I told you, Annie, that girl is after him."

"They're just dancing, Jill," I said.

"And that's what we should be doing." Peter pulled me onto the floor. Suddenly trapped in the crush of hips and elbows, we swayed together for a moment trying to get our balance, but I was stiff in his arms.

"Hey, will you forget about Christina?"

The deejay was playing something slow. I nestled against his chest, trying to relax. Being with him was all that mattered. I rubbed my cheek against his shirt, rested my ear at his heart. His fingers played on my neck, sent shivers deep into my shoulders and through my breasts. I wouldn't let myself think beyond right now.

12

I opened my eyes seconds before the crush of bone and lay there gripping the blanket at my chest, grateful to have avoided the hot pain of exploding organs I always anticipated. As usual, I'd been careening toward ground, my heart pounding and eyes struggling to open before impact. Now I stared into the dark and sighed heavily to calm my breathing.

Pull the rip cord, I'd said to myself for years before going to sleep. You've got a parachute. Use it. But periodically the dream would catch me again and I'd kick and scream through the air, too panicked to find the strap that could save me.

That night, even knowing I was safe, my body still twitched a little, unable to give up its adrenaline rush. I rolled onto my side, trying to get settled again, and was almost comfortable when something made me open my eyes and peer into the darkness toward the other bed. Christina wasn't there. I leaned forward, still hoping to make out a shape under the covers, but there was just the blanket and sheet pushed back to form a ragged wall across the middle of the bed.

I lay there a moment, waiting to hear sounds from the bathroom, the creak of a certain floorboard in the hall, the slight movement of my door being gently opened and closed. Nothing. The house was quiet except for the slight vibrating hum of my clock. I glanced at its face. Three-fifteen. Where could she be in the middle of the night? I lay there another minute, reluctant to desert my warm bed for the chill of the dark house. The silence sucked me back toward sleep, and I dozed for a moment, then awoke again with a lurch, as if the quiet held its own alarm.

There was nothing to do but find her, so I crawled out of bed, wishing I had on a heavy granny gown instead of one of Greg's T-shirts. At least I was still wearing socks. I considered searching for my robe in the pile of clothes on the closet floor but decided it was too much trouble.

I eased the door open. The hall was even colder and darker than my room, and I hugged my arms for warmth as I tiptoed over to the landing and peered down. There were no lights below, no hissing kettle from the kitchen, just the streetlight's dim glow through the glass in the front door. The bathroom door was open and the room dark.

Where was she? I wondered. I'd have to wake Mom and Dad, but what would I say to them? That Christina had disappeared?

I was shivering as I crept along the banister, wishing someone had remembered to replace the burned-out bulb in the night-light. In the dark, my path seemed longer than the thirty feet it must have been.

At Mom and Dad's door, I raised my hand to knock, then stopped, feeling my skin prickling beneath my shirt. The air around me suddenly felt contained, as if a heavy cloak were being lifted that would fall over me if I moved. Someone was there. I could sense breathing, the quiver of flesh within reach.

"Christina?" I peered into the shadows toward the end of the L where Greg's room was, then waited breathlessly to catch movement in the dark.

Christina's face, pale in its frame of dark tumbling hair, appeared out of the corner. "Oh, you scared me so bad," she whispered, grabbing my hand.

"What's wrong?" I squeezed her fingers. "What are you doing?"

"I must have been sleepwalking," she whispered. I could feel her trembling. "When I woke up, I was standing here and I didn't know where I was. Oh, I'm so glad you found me."

We slipped past the landing. In my room, I flung a scarf over my bedside lamp and switched it on. Soft blue light fell on the rumpled beds, the cluttered dresser, Christina's ghostly, streaked face.

"Why didn't you tell me you walk in your sleep?" I asked. "You should have told me, Christina."

"I haven't done it in a long time. In years." She grabbed my hand again. "I didn't think I'd do it anymore, it's been so long. When I was in grade school I could never go to pajama parties or spend the night over because of it. It was like having a handicap or something."

"Well, I'll have to tell Mom and Dad."

"Don't, Annie, please don't." She pressed my hand to her heart before I could pull away.

"Christina, I have to." I refused to look at her eyes again; smudged with mascara, they loomed out of the shadows. "It's cold. Get back in bed."

"I thought I could trust you," Christina said

tearfully. She sat down on the bed and pulled a blanket around her shoulders but didn't lie down. "I thought we were friends."

"We are friends." I hunted around on the floor and found a cardigan sweater to put on. "But I can't lie to my parents. They trust me, Christina. You could stumble over Clancy some night. What if you fell down the stairs and got hurt?"

"I won't!" Christina sobbed. "I didn't!"

"I'm telling them," I said firmly and pulled the covers up over my legs.

Christina moaned and fell back on the bed. "Then I guess I have to tell you the truth," she said. Her voice quavered on fresh tears. "I made that up about sleepwalking because I know it'll look bad—"

"What will, Christina?" I stared at her.

"I'm so embarrassed, Annie. It's so silly—I know you'll think so. So silly and so immature, not like something you'd do at all."

"Try me." I didn't even care how impatient I sounded.

"I couldn't go to sleep," Christina said with a tremulous sigh. "I had such a fantastic time at the dance, Annie. It was so great and I guess I was too excited to sleep. Anyway, I lay here a long time, hours it seemed like, feeling like I was just going to burst if I didn't talk to somebody. I just had to say how terrific everything is, how happy I am." She paused, and when she began again, her voice was so soft I had to lean forward to hear. "I didn't want to wake you, so I thought of Greg and how we danced and everything. Of course, I know it was just part of a dance, until Amanda came back and cut in on us—I know it wasn't anything really—but I thought, maybe he can't sleep either. Maybe he's just lying there thinking about things and wishing he had somebody to talk to, just like me."

"Greg? Awake in the middle of the night?" My laugh sounded like a little bark in the quiet. "Greg has to be pulled bodily out of bed every morning of his life," I said in a hard whisper.

"I told you it was dumb. Please don't tell him I wanted to talk to him, Annie," Christina pleaded. Her voice was clear now, her spring of tears dry. "I'd die if he knew."

"And you made up all that about sleepwalking? How could you do that, Christina? How could you even think of it?"

"I don't know," Christina said. "Sometimes I just do the wrong thing, Annie. Mama says I'm like a loose cannon. She says—"

I remember thinking that it always ends up being

her mother who's really to blame. Always criticizing. Always impatient. I softened a little. "Everybody screws up sometimes."

"You won't tell, will you, Annie? I'd never be able to face your family if you do." Christina was leaning toward me, and the blue haze from the lamp spread its gauzy light across her pain-drawn face. "I'd have to give up everything."

I hesitated for a moment. What would I say, anyway? "Okay, I won't tell," I said, reaching for the light.

The sudden dark was too black to peer into, and so I closed my eyes, listening to Christina's movements on the bed, the *kusch*ing sound of the pillow as her head touched it, the soft spring of coils settling under her. I heard breathing, too, at first quick and punctuated by sighs but then the even, shallow rhythm of sleep. I looked at the clock. A little after four. Three more hours before the house would be awake, but I was as alert as if the alarm had just buzzed at my ear.

I was remembering what Jill had said about Christina liking Greg. Well, so what? Lots of girls probably liked him—why, I didn't know. But Christina was here in the house. That made it different. And tonight she was outside his room. What if I hadn't found her when I did? Or what if Mom had discovered her instead? Would Mom believe her story? Was it just a story? I didn't know.

I'll think about something else, I thought, punching the pillow tightly around my neck. I'll think about having REM show up at a party I'm having. Or winning the Publishers' Clearinghouse Sweepstakes. Or dancing with Peter. But the pictures wouldn't catch in my head. Their brightness flashed past my closed eyes, too ephemeral to hold, and for the rest of the night, there was only the memory of cold air against my legs in the dark hallway and a small plaintive voice begging me not to tell.

13

Christina was still there when Peter came to pick me up at noon. After the dance the night before, Peter and I had decided to spend most of Saturday together.

"Doing whatever you want," he'd said between a trail of tiny kisses inside the collar of my coat that had eventually ended at the edge of my mouth.

"Without Rosie?" I'd felt warm, knowing the answer already.

"Definitely." We had both been in the passenger seat of the Jeep, as close as we could get considering our down jackets and thick gloves. "The bird is out of the picture."

"I can't imagine what we'll do without her," I'd said, reaching up to kiss him.

"Well, I can." His chest had swelled against my

cheek as he sighed. "We're never alone, Annie."

"And whose fault is that?"

"We're both guilty, I guess."

"So tomorrow we'll be alone." I'd tried to sound seductive.

"Yeah." Peter had kissed me slowly, then leaned back against the seat to watch the lights of a car pulling up behind us. "It's Randy and Christina."

I pushed on the door handle. "I should go in with her. Randy's probably worried about whether or not to kiss her, and I can spare him the dilemma."

"I guess you're right. Knowing Christina, he'll probably make the wrong choice." He'd held me tightly for a second. "Tomorrow then. Alone."

And now here was Christina on the sofa folding laundry next to Greg, who was watching a pregame basketball show on television. Peter frowned in her direction before I could pull him back into the hall.

"What's she doing here?" he asked.

"She keeps saying her mom will be here any minute," I whispered.

"Then let's just leave her," Peter said.

I hesitated, haunted by the night before. "I can't do that. Nobody's home but Greg and me."

"So what does that mean?" Peter asked. "We're not wasting our day because of her, are we?"

I hugged his arm. "Sh-h-h-h. What if we take her home? Do you mind?"

"Whatever." Peter shrugged. "Just get her to come on. I should have known something like this would happen."

Christina went reluctantly. "Mom's probably on her way," she said when she dialed the number and got no answer.

"Then Greg can tell her we've given you a ride." I nudged Greg into attention.

"What? Sure," Greg said, already back with the television.

"All right then," Christina said, folding the last towel into the basket. "I guess I'll go."

We rode out into the country in silence, and when I glanced back at Christina, she looked glum, her eyes fixed on the gloomy landscape of plowed-up fields and gray sky.

"Turn here," she said finally, and Peter wheeled the Jeep onto a lane that opened after an eighth of a mile into a yard surrounded by a falling fence where a car and a truck were parked beside a dilapidated farmhouse.

"Looks like somebody's home now," Peter said.

"Maybe there's something wrong with the phone," I said.

Christina was gathering her things on the seat. "I guess so." She pulled her overnight bag and books out with her and slammed the door.

"See you Monday!" I called, but Christina had disappeared around the house without answering.

"Well, thank you very much." Peter turned the Jeep around and headed back toward the highway. "Wonder what that was all about."

"Beats me." But I was thinking about last night. "Most of the time she seems just like everybody else, and then, all of a sudden, she's really weird. I can't figure her out."

"Well, I'll have to admit she's going to be terrific in the show. Maybe she's one of those people who come alive when they get to be somebody else." He reached for my hand. "Now can we talk about something else? Please?"

I was quiet, unable to close my mind against the picture of Christina outside Greg's room. What if she'd wanted more than someone to talk to? I wished I hadn't promised not to tell.

"So. What's going on?" he asked after we'd ridden a couple of miles in silence.

"Nothing. Absolutely nothing." I hated the sullen tone in my voice, but there it was and I knew he heard it.

"So I guess there's nothing to talk about." He put both hands on the wheel as if driving suddenly took his full attention.

"Oh, come off it. You want to talk about something besides school and the play and Christina but then you don't say anything." I glared at him. "I suppose it's my job to entertain you."

"I don't expect you to entertain me, Annie. In fact, lately I don't expect much of you at all."

"That's a laugh." I stared out at the wintry afternoon, my face turned from him. Why was I picking a fight, anyway? This wasn't at all what I wanted.

"Sometimes I wish we'd just met," I said. "I mean, it would be exciting getting to know each other. We'd have all sorts of new stuff to talk about."

"And now all we've got is Christina," Peter said. "Is that the attraction—her being new?"

"You make it sound like she's a toy or something." I felt my face flush, and my throat was hot with anger. "One thing for sure, she's not dumb. She notices things nobody else seems to get—like how Amanda's all over you at rehearsals."

"Give me a break."

"She says Amanda flirts and you flirt back."

"And you listen to that garbage? Good Lord, Annie."

"Then why did she say it? There's no reason to make up something like that." I could feel the bones in my fingers when I squeezed my hands together. They felt tender, breakable.

"I don't know. I don't know anything about her and I don't care. All I know is that you're being ridiculous over nothing."

"That's what guys always say. You think you can do anything you want to. You're the man, right? And if I have an opinion you don't like, then I'm being ridiculous."

"I don't know what the hell you're talking about, Annie. All I know is you're in a funk all the time and I'm getting sick of it."

I didn't want to look at him but I couldn't stop myself now. "Well, you don't have to put up with me at all, you know. Technically, we aren't even going together."

"Technically? What kind of word is that? And just what do you call what's been happening for the past six months?" Peter was gripping the wheel, his foot pressed hard on the accelerator.

I wanted to tell him to slow down but I didn't. "I don't know. What do you call it? You've never asked me to go steady, have you? I think I'd remember that."

"We don't date other people, so I thought it was understood, but if it isn't, don't think I'm about to ask you now." He was more angry than I'd ever seen him, but he managed to slow down to take the turn back into town.

That was when a crushing panic slammed into my chest. I had never felt anything like it. "Where are we going? I thought we were doing something."

"I don't think so." He turned down Reynolds, passed his own house and pulled up in front of mine.

"You just want to run away. You just don't want any confrontation." My voice kept jumping in my throat. "Keep everything nice and light, that's what you want. Well, maybe I can't always do that."

"Yeah, Annie, you're right. You can't."

He wasn't looking at me, but I knew he was waiting for me to get out. "Maybe you don't want us to be together at all," I said, feeling a blur of hot tears.

He turned to me then, his face set stubbornly. "I didn't say that."

"Then I guess I'm saying it." I didn't even bother to shut the door behind me.

Inside, Greg was still in front of the television. Clancy stirred and went upstairs with me, nuzzling against my leg for attention, but I ignored him. My room was tidy, the beds changed, my laundry put away. Christina's doing. I plopped facedown on the bed and heard Clancy settling on the floor nearby. I was trembling and I pressed my arms between my chest and the bed, holding myself still. What had I done? What? I hadn't meant it, not any of it. It was like someone else had been talking, somebody else who was sullen and angry and vengeful.

He'll call me, I reasoned. He'll know I didn't mean it. He'll see it was just a fight. People fight all the time, right? He'll call. I just have to wait. I went to sleep thinking that.

It was dark when I awoke. Clancy had gone and I could smell dinner cooking. The television was still on downstairs. I went to the bathroom and washed my face and brushed my hair. I looked drugged. I hadn't slept the night before. That was the reason for all this. I'd promised Christina I wouldn't tell, but I should have told Peter. He wasn't family. I'd tell him now.

I went back to my room and pressed the numbers in the dark.

"Why, he's not here, Annie," Ms. Hughes said.

"He left a few minutes ago, so he should be on your doorstep by now."

"Thanks," I said and pressed Jill's number.

"She's gone out," Dr. Tatum said. "I think she's with Peter Hughes. Just a minute." He was back on the phone immediately. "Anne, her mom says she just left with Peter, so they should be at your house before you know it."

I put down the phone and sat there, holding my arms and shoulders stiff. They would be here any minute. Of course they would. I would wait. Peter had convinced Jill to be his emissary and they were on their way. I would sit absolutely still, not disturbing anything, holding steady until I heard the doorbell. I could do that. In my mind, I willed the ringing bell, the door opening, Jill's voice calling, their footsteps on the stairs coming to get me.

I bent suddenly at the waist, holding back a cry. It was almost seven. Nobody had phoned. They weren't coming.

Downstairs I could hear Martha laughing, a broadcaster's artificial phrasing, Mom calling us to dinner. I couldn't eat but I couldn't explain either. Not yet, not before I understood it myself. I would have to go down and pretend.

"Oh God, oh no." My voice frightened me with

its helpless whine. Where were they? What were they doing without me?

"Anne!" It was Mom. "Annie, dinner's ready!"

"Coming!" I would have to get through dinner somehow. I'd get through the evening, too, without giving my family any reason to console me. That way it wouldn't be true, although my stomach already ached with abandonment. I felt the pressure of it like a weight on my chest that could stop my breath. How could this hurt be so sudden, so overwhelming? I wondered.

I don't have anybody, I thought suddenly, struck through with a pain that made me moan aloud. What would I do without Peter and Jill? How could I survive without knowing they needed me? Who was I without them?

It had always been Jill who needed me. She was the one who always wanted to make plans in advance, to have assurance that she wouldn't be alone on weekends.

"She doesn't know what to do with herself," I'd heard Ms. Tatum say to Mom when we were in grade school. "Why, the child can't be alone ten minutes."

"She just has so much energy," Mom had said to console her. "Besides, little girls love theatrics. I was that way myself, always making something happen."

Maybe it didn't really matter to Jill who she was with as long as she had somebody.

"Chow time, Annie," Greg called from downstairs. "We're eating."

I pulled myself up again. "I'm coming! Just a minute!"

Before I knew it, he was in the doorway. "What's up, Sis?"

"Nothing." I turned toward him with a smile that felt too fragile to be convincing but he had already disappeared.

"Everything's fine," I said, testing my voice, and then I followed him down, determined to make it so.

14

I faked period cramps to stay home from church, but after the family left, I couldn't stay in bed. Down in the kitchen, I heated the last of the coffee in the microwave and took it into the living room, clicked on the TV, and sat staring at the morning movie without the volume on. The actors, none of whom I recognized, looked like robots, their gestures stupid and affected.

I felt mute myself and I watched the colored forms mindlessly, my brain too fuzzy to care what they were doing. My belly did ache, a slight dull throbbing low in my groin. Maybe that was the reason for yesterday. I sipped the coffee, then pressed the hot base of the mug to my stomach. Emma curved herself into a golden orb and settled against my knee.

The phone rang but I didn't get up to answer it. Everybody knew we went to church. After the phone stopped ringing, it occurred to me that maybe the caller was a burglar casing the house, so I made myself get up and check the doors.

My folks weren't home when the phone rang again, so this time I struggled off the sofa to answer it.

"Annie, what's up?" It was Jill. She was her usual exuberant self but I detected a nervous edge in her tone. "I thought I'd see you at church."

Hearing her voice brought a quick flood of heat to my cheeks. "Cramps."

"Yuk. Sorry." Jill paused, then spun on. "Listen, we've got lots to talk about. Do you think you'll feel like getting together later this afternoon?"

"What for?"

"Were you asleep?" Jill went on without waiting for an answer. "You sound funny. You're not zonked on Midol, are you?"

"I'm fine. What do we have to talk about?"

"The debate stuff, of course. Dan said he could come over here. Phoebe, too. We need a meeting before tomorrow if you and Dan are going to talk to Ms. Fletcher."

I said, "I can talk to Dan about it on the phone.

I don't think we need a meeting."

"Oh." The line was silent for a moment. "Well, if you don't think we do, that's fine. Listen, Annie, I wanted to talk to you about something else, anyway. I know you and Peter had a fight. He told me. He was at church this morning."

"This morning? That's when he told you? And what did he tell you last night, Jill?" My voice was so icy I hardly recognized it. "I know you went out with him, so don't deny it."

"I'm not denying anything."

There was a deep silence, as if a hole had opened up between us, but I didn't try to fill it.

"I wouldn't call it going out," Jill said finally.

"Then what would you call it? I thought you were my friend," I said. "My best friend."

"I thought I was, too. Until lately." I could hear her breathing. "Annie, just what are you accusing me of?"

"You tell me."

"I don't have anything to tell. I haven't done anything wrong," Jill said. "And if you think I have, then what kind of friend are you, anyway?"

"Maybe you don't want us to be friends anymore."

"Annie, what's the matter with you?"

"Nothing. "

"Well, you're acting crazy. I've known Peter as long as you have. The three of us have been buddies forever."

"And last night you went out with him. You didn't call me or anything."

"Well, I'm calling you now."

"It's a little late, don't you think?"

"Annie, you're losing it, do you know that?" Jill was practically shouting into the phone, then she was quiet as if someone had come into the room. I wondered if Peter was there with her. "Just think about it and you'll see how stupid it is. I'll see you at school tomorrow."

I hung up without responding and stayed at the counter, looking out the window at the bright winter morning. It would be a good day to fly Rosie.

The house was painfully quiet. I wished everybody would come home. Maybe when all of them were in the kitchen making lunch I'd feel better. I needed their voices around me, the comforting smell of Mom's cheese soup simmering. Well, I could get it started.

I got out the leftover soup and ladled it into a pot, then sliced part of a turkey breast for sandwiches. I was setting the table when the phone rang again. It was Dad.

"How're you feeling?" he wanted to know.

"Better," I said, although hearing his concern made me teary. "I'm up."

"Well, we've decided to go out for lunch," Dad said. "We'll swing by and pick you up if you'd like."

I turned away from the phone to clear my voice.

"Are you sure you're okay, sweetheart?" he was asking me.

"I'm fine. But I don't feel like going out. You guys go ahead, though."

"Mom says there's soup in the fridge. We'll be home by two or so."

"Okay, Dad."

I tried not to think while I put the food away and cleared the table. Upstairs I stood in the shower letting the water jet across my aching breasts and belly. The spray was almost unbearably hot. I didn't adjust it but stood there breathing in the thick steam and feeling the burning splash of water.

When I dried off, I was streaked with heat, my fingers and toes white and shriveled. The bathroom was so steamy I felt faint, so, wrapped in a towel, I went out into the hall, and leaned against the wall to breathe the cool, dry air.

From there I could see four bedrooms wrapped

around the stairwell, each of them enclosing the essence of the people who owned them: the odd things they'd saved, the books they were reading, the clothing they wore, the secrets they had hidden. There was my room, too, the only room I could remember having. This was the only house I could remember, too. Why am I so lonely here? I wondered, feeling the chill now after the heat of the bathroom. How could it be that what I needed most was somewhere else, outside the safety of these walls?

I wanted Peter. I wanted his voice telling me everything we'd said was forgiven, even forgotten, that we could go on like always. We had all this history together, all these years that had to count for something. You just didn't give it up. Maybe I should call Jill. She was my best friend. We knew everything about each other. Jill would never intentionally hurt me.

But going out with Peter was the kind of thing she'd do without thinking because she was vaguely self-centered and spoiled the way kids are whose parents have no reason to deny them anything. It's not her fault she's an only child, I thought.

But Christina was an only child, too, now that her brother had died, and she didn't seem privileged. Christina knew about sadness. She had been lonely, bereft of her boyfriend, her old neighborhood and school, even her father temporarily. Maybe she acted weird sometimes, but she would know this pain that made me grimace, bearing down as I leaned against the wall, still wrapped in a cold towel.

I went to my room and closed the door, slipped into my robe and lay down on the bed. It took me only moments to decide. I fumbled in the bedside table drawer, searching for the paper on which Christina had written her number, studied the digits for another second, and then pressed them on the dial pad. The phone rang only once before someone picked it up. "Hello?" The voice was small, expectant, maybe even a little surprised.

"Christina? It's Annie." We sounded the same.

15

I did what I always used to do when things went wrong—made myself too busy to think. The next morning before homeroom, I was waiting for Dan at his locker.

"I just made an appointment for the two of us with Ms. Fletcher for today during lunch." I tried to sound calm but my breath was shuddering heavily. It sounded like sighs.

"Chill out, Annie," Dan said, without looking at me. He was trying to keep the junk in his locker from spilling out while he searched for a notebook. "I haven't seen my history notes in a week and we've got a test tomorrow."

I tried for a deep breath again and felt it push against the book bag I was clutching to my chest. I didn't want to tell Dan the meeting with Ms.

Fletcher wasn't my biggest worry. What I dreaded more was seeing Peter. And what about Jill? How was I supposed to act around them? Would they pretend nothing had happened?

"Hi." It was Jill behind me at her locker.

"Hi," Dan said, smiling at her over my head. "Annie's made an appointment with Fletcher for noon."

"Great," Jill said without much enthusiasm.

I could hear her cramming books into her locker. I knew how messy it was without looking. I didn't want to look, anyway. How many times had I been the one to find things Jill had misplaced? I'd always organized study sessions for us, explained the subtleties of movie plots, shown her how to do the same algebra assignment three times before she even paid attention. Well, Jill was scatterbrained—that was one of the reasons I loved her. But she was stubborn, too. And spoiled.

"Well, see you later," Jill said to Dan. I could hear her move away.

"What's with you two?" Dan wanted to know.

"Nothing," I said, although a hot bubble was exploding in my chest and my fingers ached like I was trying to strangle my book bag. "Don't forget we're going to the office after English class. And will you try to get organized, Dan? We can't just go in there and blubber."

"Whoa, Annie, don't take it out on me." Dan was still rummaging through his locker. "Here it is!" He pulled a ragged notebook out of the clutter. "Thank God! I thought I was going to have to copy yours." He slammed the metal door.

"Fat chance," I said when he'd left me standing there.

ೋ

So this is how it's going to be, I thought. Jill was sitting across the aisle from me, close enough to touch, but her shoulder was turned away, her profile partially hidden by her hair while she did her French homework. The school secretary was reading the announcements with her mouth too close to the microphone, so her voice blared and her breath made rumbling, staticky slices in the air. There would be an Honor Society meeting during homeroom tomorrow, the revised *Kiss Me, Kate* schedule was on the band room board, there was a pep rally planned for Friday.

Peter would be there, he would be everywhere. So would Jill. My breath matched the secretary's, as loud and cringing as that. They were my life. Who would I sit with at the rally? What would I do in biology lab this afternoon if Jill wouldn't talk to me? What about lunch?

The curl of panic in my stomach tightened again, my mouth went dry. I wanted to reach out and touch Jill's shoulder, but what if it was stiff, un-yielding? I could imagine a stony, unrelenting face turned to me, a "no" already formed in the hard set of her mouth.

This isn't fair, I thought. Jill's the one who ought to apologize, but of course she's too dumb to know it. Too spoiled, too, so it's just like her to think somebody else is to blame.

I tightened my hands in my lap. Of course, they probably just went for a pizza and Peter talked about me the whole time. He wanted someone to commiserate with and naturally he picked Jill. Who else could he talk to?

Then why hadn't Jill convinced him to call? Didn't she know we'd argued because we were tired? Surely she knew it didn't mean anything. I'd read in one of Mom's magazines that couples were apt to fight on weekends because it was the only time they could slow down enough to consider grievances. When I got a chance, I'd tell Peter that. I'd say I understood how the whole thing happened.

But why did I have to be the one to apologize?

My heart was pounding just like it had the night before; it filled my chest with the memory of how I'd felt knowing they were together without me. If Peter wanted to work it out, it was up to him—after all, he'd taken me home in the middle of an argument. Anyway, he was smart. He didn't need Jill's advice about anything.

My stomach knotted, released, knotted again. Oh, I missed him! I even missed Jill, who was sitting there beside me, pretending to wrestle with French conjugations. I envisioned the day spreading out in front of me, a long lonely spiral of hours, an evening without the phone ringing. They had no right to do this to me. Why shouldn't I force a confrontation if that was what it took?

"Jill. Hey, Jill," I whispered, but the first bell blared, covering my voice, and Jill was out the door as if she hadn't heard.

ε∂

In the principal's office, Dan and I sat on the straight chairs Ms. Fletcher offered us.

"So what's the problem?" She was smiling as she came around to lean against the front of her desk. "I know there must be one for you two to give up lunch."

I glanced at Dan, both irritated and relieved that

he looked blank, as if he, too, were wondering what the issue was. At least he's here, I thought. Don't think about Jill and Peter, I reminded myself. I could handle this without them. I didn't need them at all.

"We're here about our English class," I began, then waited for Ms. Fletcher to react. Dad had warned me that principals probably didn't get curriculum complaints from students very often so I should try to move carefully and concisely to the point.

"Oh?" If Ms. Fletcher was surprised, she didn't show it, but she did settle in her chair again and drew a notepad in front of her. "Which English class is that?"

"Ms. Langley's fourth period," Dan said firmly, as if this were his important contribution.

"We're reading *Julius Caesar*," I added.

"It's pretty good, too," Dan said, warming to his task a little.

I felt suddenly flushed. What if my family were brought into this? Not that Mom would mind. I would, though.

Dan was going on. "Anyway, we were discussing Shakespeare, you know, as a person, and it came up somehow that Shakespeare might not be Shakespeare. At least, some people think that—" He stopped, giving me a chance to take over.

"So we decided to have a debate about it," I said. "We divided into teams and we've been doing research."

Ms. Fletcher hadn't written anything yet.

I kept going. "The problem is that Mr. Johnson told Ms. Langley we can't have the debate, but we think we should be able to go ahead with it. We should be able to discuss anything we want to."

"Anything?" Ms. Fletcher asked.

"Anything relevant." I felt breathless. Maybe I'd said too much. "We're here about the right to open inquiry." That was Mom's phrase. "About intellectual freedom."

"We just want to have the debate," Dan said.

Ms. Fletcher was taking notes now. After a moment she looked up, her pencil resting on the pad. "I have to tell you I usually don't interfere in curriculum matters. That's why we have departmental committees in a school this size. But I will look into it and get back to you in a few days."

"In another week, we'll be finished with *Julius Caesar*," I said.

"I can't tell you exactly which day," Ms. Fletcher answered firmly, "but I'll notify you after

I've talked to Mr. Johnson and Ms. Langley. Now you'd better go on to lunch or you'll miss it altogether." She stood up. "By the way," she said, opening the door for us, "how's the play going?"

"Fine," I said.

"Yeah, it's okay," Dan said.

"Well, I'm looking forward to it," Ms. Fletcher said with a smile.

❧

Instead of going to the cafeteria, I looked for Christina in the theater arts room. She was playing one of the Chopin études I still stumbled through.

"That's nice," I said, sitting down on the bench with her.

"I miss my piano so much." Christina let her hands slide off the keys.

"You can play ours anytime you'd like." I could remember being irritated with her in this very room, but now that seemed like years ago.

"You had the meeting?" Christina asked. "I thought you'd be in the cafeteria telling everybody."

"Dan's doing it. I came to tell you." I played a few bars of treble chords, a miniature fanfare. "Ms. Fletcher said she'd look into it and get back to us in a few days."

"Then I think we should go ahead with the

petition," Christina said. "I don't trust her one bit."

"You don't even know her."

"She's an adult, right? And she's the boss. Don't you think she'll support the establishment? You bet she will." Christina riffed through a boogie-woogie bass.

"Not all adults are like that," I said, but suddenly I felt defeated. Maybe the meeting hadn't gone well after all. Maybe Ms. Fletcher had no intention of doing anything. "I need to get something to eat."

"I've got an apple and a slice of pumpkin bread I was saving for after school. You can have that."

"I can't take your snack," I said, but the thought of going into the cafeteria was making me squeamish.

"Of course you can." Christina handed me a crumpled sack. "What are best friends for?"

16

That afternoon at rehearsal, Ms. Dalton told us we'd be practicing four afternoons a week and the next two Saturdays. "We'll try to be finished by one o'clock," she said. "Of course, that depends on you."

"Sure it does," Dan mumbled beside me.

"Complete orchestra rehearsals start tomorrow," Mr. Dorsey announced. "That means everybody!"

"Let's get serious now!" Ms. Dalton boomed. "This show has the potential to be the best production we've ever done, but to achieve that we have to have total concentration and dedication from here on."

"A final word from Tweedledee and Tweedledum," Christina whispered behind us.

"Hardly," Dan said. "That woman's final word

will be two seconds before the opening curtain."

I was scanning the crowd for Peter.

"He's backstage with Amanda," Christina whispered at my shoulder. How did she always know what I was thinking? "I guess that's where I should be, too. See you later."

Wishing for the first time that I had a stage part, I headed back to the band room with the rest of the orchestra. My whole day seemed contrived to isolate me.

On my way to the band room, I met Ms. Langley under the breezeway. "There you are, Annie." She looked tired and upset. "We need to talk. Can you come to my office for a minute?"

"For a minute. I'm supposed to be at rehearsal." I followed her into the building.

She started talking as soon as she'd closed the door behind us. "I just had a meeting with Ms. Fletcher. She called me in about the debate. I didn't know you and Dan were going to see her."

"We thought you'd try to stop us—"

"And I would have. I was disappointed, Annie, you know that, but this debate is not so important that I'm willing to risk my job over it."

"But you're not risking anything," I said. "That's why we decided not to tell you—so you wouldn't be responsible."

Ms. Langley sighed and sat down at her desk. "You kids just don't want to be told no about anything. That's it, isn't it? Challenge you and you're ready to do battle, no matter what the fight or the cost."

"It's a matter of intellectual freedom," I said stonily. "It doesn't have anything to do with Shakespeare anymore."

"I'm opposed to censorship, Annie. Surely you know that. But I think we all need to be careful about picking our fights."

"Mr. Johnson handed us this issue, Ms. Langley. We didn't go looking for it. I didn't want to get into the Shakespeare question to begin with. Christina Moore brought it up, remember? Then you suggested the debate and we got excited about it. You can't expect us to back down without a fight."

Ms. Langley frowned, rubbing her hand across her forehead. "I suppose not. But I can't help you, Annie. Whatever Ms. Fletcher decides, that'll be it." She brightened a little. "So what else do you have on your agenda? I know a visit to the principal isn't all."

"There'll be a letter to the editor in tomorrow's

paper. And tonight we're getting a petition ready to pass around school." I tried to smile. "Don't worry, Ms. Langley. We've got it under control."

But back in the band room with the ragged orchestra struggling through "So in Love," I felt myself sinking. I wasn't sure about anything anymore.

ॐ

That evening Mom and I sat at the kitchen table having the last of the apple cobbler while we worked on the petition statement. The house was quiet around us, the wintry night still against the dark windows.

"So what's happening with you?" Mom asked when we'd decided on the wording of the petition. "And don't say nothing. Something's been bothering you all weekend."

Caught off guard, I felt a rush of tears and I sipped my coffee to keep from speaking too soon. This is how it should be, I thought. Mom and me alone like this, talking about stuff. But what could I tell her? About Christina outside Greg's room? About my fight with Peter? About him and Jill closing me out?

"Peter and I had an argument Saturday and I haven't seen him since," I said finally. I couldn't stop the tears. Now there was no faking it. "He hasn't even called me, Mom, and I don't think he's going to," I sobbed. "Jill's mad with me, too. And Ms. Langley's upset because I went to see the principal. Everything I do is wrong! Everything!"

Mom got up to get the tissue box and, when she returned, put her arms around my shoulders from the back, resting her chin on my head. "Oh, Annie," she said softly. "What a hard time."

"Thank goodness for Christina. She's turning out to be the only friend I've got." I wiped my eyes and blew into a tissue. "What's wrong with me, Mom?"

"Nothing, sweetheart."

"Well, it's either me or them. Something's wrong somewhere."

"Maybe you should call Peter yourself. Jill, too. If you miss them, why not?"

"I don't know. I want to! But I can't make myself. It hurts too much, Mom."

"But it's your pride that's hurt, isn't it? I don't know what's happened, but I know if you want it fixed, you'd better do something about it yourself."

"But why do I have to be responsible for everything? The orchestra sounds terrible, the debate's in limbo."

"All of that will work itself out. We'll enjoy the

show no matter how the orchestra sounds. And maybe the debate won't happen. We'll be sorry— I'll be furious, but—" She shrugged, then began gathering the dishes from the table.

"But what about Jill and Peter?" I felt tears again. "They're so important to me, Mom."

"Then I guess you'll figure out what to do about it," she said.

>

"Peter?" It was hard not to cry at the sound of his voice.

"Annie?"

"Yes."

"God, I'm glad you called." His voice seemed muffled.

"I thought I'd see you today."

"I know. Me, too. Things just got so crazy at school; then I tried to call you a little while ago but the line was busy."

"Martha thinks she owns it." I could sense his smile.

"So, what's up?" he asked.

"Nothing." I tried to keep from breathing hard into the phone. "I'd better warn you, the orchestra is awful."

"Well, we're not so hot either. I hear you and

Dan had a meeting with Ms. Fletcher. Good for you, Annie."

"I thought it went okay, but now I don't know." My voice trailed off and there was silence.

"Hey listen, I'll see you tomorrow," Peter said finally. "At lunch. Let's 'do' lunch, okay?" He sounded buoyant.

"Okay." I waited, forcing courage. "Peter, I'm sorry about Saturday."

"Me, too," he said. "We'll talk about it tomorrow."

I felt better, but there was still Jill to think about. I lay there wondering why I was more angry with her than with Peter. After all, Peter must have called her. She should have called me, though. Maybe Peter needed time to chill out, but Jill didn't. She had to have known how I was feeling. At least, if she weren't in la-la land most of the time, she'd have known.

I pressed her number, but the line was busy. Every five minutes from ten thirty till eleven, I punched the redial button but the phone was never free. Finally I curled up under the covers and switched off the light. Mom and Dad were still up. I could hear the television in their bedroom; the weatherman was giving his report for tomorrow. I wondered vaguely what he was saying. Temperatures in the thirties for the rest of the week? Cloudy skies? A chance of snow?

I snuggled deeper into the warmth I'd made. It didn't matter about the weather. Inside I felt that old heat, a surge of energy rekindled. Tomorrow I'd find a way to fix everything.

ॐ

The petition started around the school even before the newspaper came out, and by noon there were more than a hundred names.

"Of course, some people signed it without reading it," Dan said in the cafeteria line.

"And some wouldn't sign at all," Phoebe said. "The jerks."

"Some people don't want to risk any kind of trouble," Jill said.

"And some people can't resist taking it on," Peter added, nudging me with his shoulder.

I took courage. "I tried to call you last night, Jill."

"You did?" Jill eyed the tuna salads instead of me. She finally selected one. "Oh, I bet I was on the phone with Christina. She wants to help plan the cast party."

"Since when?" I tried not to show surprise. Ms.

Tatum and Mom had planned last year's party.

"Since yesterday." Jill still hadn't looked my way. "Ms. Fletcher said we could have it right here in the cafeteria as long as we have enough parents and faculty to keep it contained."

"Yeah, she's into containment," Dan said.

"Sounds great." I frowned at the grilled cheese sandwiches on the hot tray in front of me.

"Yeah, well, I didn't say anything yesterday because—because you had all that Shakespeare junk on your mind." Jill had that awkward half smile on her face; then she turned away. "Look at that, somebody's got our table!"

"I didn't know we had our names on it," Dan said. They went to find another place.

"Let's sit somewhere else," Peter said.

I gave him a grateful smile.

"I want to talk to you," he went on, sounding serious.

My hand was actually trembling when I set my glass of milk on the tray. My mind skittered through all the possibilities. He's going to tell me it's all over between us. Last night didn't mean anything. He doesn't need me anymore. That's what our relationship was about, anyway. Need. When he was skinny and awkward and too smart, nobody really liked him but me. But now he has everything—the starring role in the play and friends, more friends than I have—and it's over between us.

The only empty table was on the far wall, and I had to maneuver around chairs and tables to get to it. The cafeteria was loud with talk and laughter, clanging trays and sliding chairs, but the noise seemed at a distance. I could hear only my internal roaring.

"So," Peter said, settling his tray across from mine. He sat down and studied his food for a moment.

Now, I said silently, hurt me if you can. Because my heart was closing up, solidifying against a blow. His hand came across the table, held palm up, softly curled, waiting.

What is this? I wondered but, unable to resist his touch, laid my hand in his.

His fingers curled, squeezed, softened again. "I missed you," he said, and put my fingers to his lips.

17

So everything was going to be all right, wasn't it? It didn't matter that the orchestra sounded awful or that the debate was in limbo or even that Jill and I were still at odds. We'd been friends too long not to work our problems out eventually. Right now I had Peter, and he was enough.

"Christina's going to be staying on Wednesday afternoons," I said after dinner while Greg and I were putting the dishes in the dishwasher. He was rinsing while I arranged.

"Why doesn't she just move in?" he asked, sloshing water on the counter between us. "I mean, she's here all the time anyway."

"She is not!" I backed up to push against him with my hip, and he flipped the dripping scrub brush at me.

"Will you two cut it out?" Mom said. "I'm not cleaning up after you!"

"The mess you make is the mess you clean!" we mocked in unison.

"All right, I mean it." Mom was trying to be stern.

"Oh no, she means it, Greg!"

"I know, I know," he said. "She always means it." He sprayed a plate and held it out to me. "What's-her-name is always here, though."

"Her name is Christina. Repeat after me—Chris-ti-na."

"Well, whatever. All I know is something about her gives me the willies," Greg said.

"Who does?" Martha asked, coming in with her math book. "Mom, I need help."

"Honey, you know I can't do simple arithmetic. Ask your dad."

"He said ask you. He said maybe you'd learn something," Martha said, trying not to smile. "Anyway, who gives you the willies, Greg? I bet it's Amanda!"

"Nobody," I said.

"Christina," Greg said.

"Oh, I love her!" Martha laid her book on the table. "Did I tell you she promised to help me with a song for the talent show Friday night?"

"She won't be here Friday night, squirt," I said. "That's the one afternoon we don't have rehearsal."

"But you're having rehearsal Saturday morning, right?" Martha said happily. She was glad she could tell us something for a change. "And Christina said this afternoon that she couldn't come to rehearsal on Saturday and what was she going to do, so I said she could spend the night with us. She can, can't she, Mom? I've already said she could."

"See what I mean?" Greg asked. "She's like a 'haint.' Once the house has her, it has to keep her." Contorting his best monster face, he moved eerily toward Martha.

"Make him stop, Mom!" Martha cried, holding her book in front of her face.

"Greg, that's gross," Mom said.

"Mom!" Martha squealed, then jumped into Greg's arms with a burst of giggles.

"I'm going out with Peter Friday night. So I won't be here with Christina," I said over the ruckus. "I didn't invite her, Mom."

"Well, it's no problem," Mom said. "We'll take her to the basketball game with us, or if she and Martha don't want to go, they can stay here. I'll run them to the video store before we leave."

"That's great, Mom," Martha said, collapsing in Greg's arms. "We'll stay here and make popcorn and watch movies and Christina can help me find the perfect song. It'll be so cool."

"If she wants to do that," I said. "I hope she doesn't expect me to stay home with her."

"She doesn't want you to and neither do I," Martha said. "Christina's a lot more fun than you are, Annie. Besides, she likes me."

"We like you, too, monkey," Greg said, hugging her, "as long as you stay in your cage."

๑

Before homeroom on Thursday, I left the signed petition with the office secretary. "Oh, Annie," the woman said, "I have a note here asking you and Dan Coleman to see Ms. Fletcher immediately after the last bell this afternoon."

"You mean she's already decided?" I asked. "But she hasn't seen the petition yet. We have almost two hundred signatures."

The woman motioned for me to come closer. "She's talked to everybody involved, including Ms. Martinez. And Ms. Langley twice," she whispered. "But I'll see she gets these this morning." She patted the papers on her desk.

At lunchtime, I raced to the cafeteria with the

news. "We have a meeting this afternoon with Ms. Fletcher," I said when the gang was at the table.

"What does that mean?" Phoebe asked. "Has she seen the petition?"

"By now she has, but I'm not very optimistic," I said.

"Well, if Ms. Fletcher says no, it's over," Jill said. "It's not like we were really going to decide something and, as far as I'm concerned, we've all got enough to do, anyway. I mean, who cares?"

"Annie does," Peter said.

"Yeah, Jill. So do I. What's wrong with you? A few days ago you were gung-ho," Phoebe said.

"Well, now all I want is the best cast party this school has ever seen!" Jill brightened. "Okay, who's got neat parents? You know, people who'll stay in the kitchen and let it happen?"

"I don't want mine here," Dan said. "It's like taking them on a date."

"Well, I don't do anything on a date my parents couldn't see," Jill said.

"At least not yet, you don't," Dan said, tousling her hair.

"Dan!" Jill cried, blushing. "You guys, ignore him, please! How about your folks, Annie? And yours, Peter?"

"I'll ask." I poked at my salad.

"Me too." When I looked up, Peter was smiling at me.

"Now, we'll need people to bring things. Cookies, chips and dip, drinks," Jill said. "Christina's mother is bringing lots of chips and she said she'd help chaperone, too. Randy's parents are bringing something and so are yours, Phoebe. What about your mom's brownies, Annie?"

"I said I'd ask, Jill. It's a month away."

"Well, you don't have to get huffy about it," Jill said. "I know a silly old cast party pales beside serious stuff like Shakespeare."

"Oh, come off it, Jill." My chair screeched when I pushed it backward. "My folks will be here and somebody will make the stupid brownies."

"Annie." Peter started to get up.

"No, stay. Eat your lunch. I'm just going to get some air."

"But it's snowing," he protested, but I went anyway.

≥▲

I found Christina leaning against the brick wall under the breezeway. She was watching the snow fall. "Aren't you freezing?" I dug my gloved hands into my parka pockets and hunched forward beside her.

"No," Christina said softly. "Listen to how quiet it is."

We were still for a moment. There was no movement but our frosty breaths.

"I wish they'd cancel school," I said. "I'd love to go home and curl up by the fire and forget everything."

"Why? What's happened?" Christina asked.

"Dan and I have a meeting with Ms. Fletcher at three." I almost told her about bolting from the cafeteria, but it seemed too silly. How could I explain Jill and me, anyway? "Jill's busy planning the cast party," I said finally.

"That's about her speed," Christina said.

"She said you were helping her."

"I guess," Christina said. "I mean, it's easier to help than not to."

"She said your mom is helping, too."

"Maybe." Christina breathed deeply and exhaled a shimmering cloud. "Don't you think snow's the saddest thing?" she said softly. "It's like the whole world's a tomb. Everything's all cold and dead."

I knew she was thinking about her brother. "Oh, but it's beautiful, too." I put my arm around her shoulder. "Stay over tonight and we'll go sledding. We've got the only hill in town."

"I don't know."

It occurred to me that she would make a perfect tragic heroine. "We'll all go—Martha, Greg, Dad— even Mom if we nag her enough. It'll be fun."

"Okay, I'll stay," Christina said, but she didn't seem especially glad.

> ❧

At three, Ms. Fletcher ushered Dan and me into her office and closed the door. "Well, I've made a decision," she said, motioning to the chairs we should sit on. "It was not an easy one, I assure you, and no matter what you might think, I did weigh all sides. I read the newspaper article and looked over the petition as well." She looked grim.

Dan glanced at me. Her decision seemed obvious to both of us.

"But Ms. Fletcher—" I tried to conjure up another argument.

"No, wait, Anne. Hear me out. I spoke to Mr. Johnson. He's not opposed to debates and certainly he believes in intellectual freedom, as do we all. But he is opposed to valuable class time being used in this way. As I'm sure you know, he considers this Shakespeare question lacking in merit."

"We do know but—"

Ms. Fletcher put up her hand to stop me. "I

spoke to Ms. Martinez, who expressed the opinion that Ms. Langley is an exemplary teacher." Her smile was dry and pinched. "Of course, I've spoken to Ms. Langley as well and she assures me that the Shakespeare unit can be a successful endeavor without this debate. She admires, as do I, the enthusiasm you've shown for the project, but she's willing to accept the chairman's decision." She cleared her throat, her hand pressed to her chest for a moment before she went on. "So my position has not been altered since we met on Monday. I don't believe in interfering with departmental curriculum affairs unless absolutely necessary, and in this particular case, I don't believe it is necessary. So"—she paused, but we knew we were not to speak—"Mr. Johnson's decision stands. No class time will be spent on the debate. Now, if you have any questions, this is the time to ask them."

"We don't have any questions," Dan said. He was staring at me, but I wasn't budging. "We've got rehearsal, Annie."

"Ah, yes." Suddenly Ms. Fletcher offered us a pleasant, relaxed smile. "Jill Tatum and her friend were in earlier about the cast party. I'm glad to say you'll be able to use the cafeteria."

"Thank you." I stood up. Dan had me by the

arm, trying to coax me away.

"Yeah, thanks," he said, closing the door behind us. "Good grief, Annie, I thought you were going to explode."

"Who, me?" I moved out of his grip and forced a smile toward the secretary on my way out. "I'm not upset," I said in the hall.

"Well, I don't know why not," Dan said, hurrying to keep up.

"Because." I stopped to link my arm in his. "We're going to do it anyway."

18

"So Ms. Fletcher wimped out," Greg said at dinner. "What did you expect?"

"Victory, of course," I said.

"Well, now the decision's been made, so let's forget about it." Dad helped himself from the salad bowl.

"I don't know," I said. "Should we let Mr. Johnson get away with this?"

"Something about kicking a dead horse comes to mind," Dad said.

"But what if this horse isn't quite dead?" I asked.

"I knew you weren't giving up!" Christina said, her face glowing.

"So what are you planning?" Mom asked. I could hear the excitement in her voice.

"We could have the debate anyway. Ms. Fletcher said we couldn't do it on school time, but what about after school or on a weekend?"

"You could have it in the fellowship hall of the church," Mom said. "I'm sure John Carlyle would agree. He'd probably even moderate. Or we could find someone at the university." She was looking at Dad.

"I vote for dropping it," he said.

"Maybe nobody will come, but at least we will have done it," I said.

"*You* will have done it, but what about everybody else?" Greg asked. "Doing all that work for a grade is one thing, but for nothing—"

Dad broke in. "I agree. It's going to take a lot of energy, plus a lot of time and emotional wear and tear on everybody. The school's going to know about this, Annie."

"My goodness, Larry, we want the school to know about it," Mom said. "I think we ought to get it on television!"

"I give up." Dad took his empty plate to the sink. "You guys can scheme all you want to. I've got better things to do."

Mom ignored him, but it was obvious she was irritated.

"Martha, it's your night to do the dishes."

"But I've got math homework, Mom. It's going to take hours!" Martha protested.

"Well, the hours will have to start after kitchen duty," Mom said firmly.

"I could take her turn," Christina offered. "If that's all right."

"Well." Mom was studying Martha's plaintive face. "Well, this one time, but that means getting to your math immediately, young lady. No talking on the phone, and no music until it's done."

"But music helps!" Martha protested. "Annie, Greg, tell her music helps."

"Music helps," I said as unconvincingly as possible.

"Yeah, Mom, it helps," Greg said, pushing back his plate with a sigh.

"You all don't care a thing about me!" Martha cried. "Nobody cares about me but Christina!"

"That's because you're not her little sister," I said. Everybody laughed except Christina.

&

On Saturday, Mom and Martha picked up Christina and me after rehearsal and took us to the mall in Lawrence. It was after two when we got there.

"Let's eat lunch before we shop," Martha said. "I'm starving."

We stopped in the Food Court and ordered sandwiches from the deli. "So what's the plan?" Mom asked while we were eating.

"I need pants," I said. "Stirrup pants, maybe. I'm sick of jeans."

"I'll go with you then," Mom said. "What about you two?"

"The music store," Martha said. "And Woolworth's, of course."

"What about the toy store?" I asked. "She still loves the toy store."

"I do not!" Martha said.

"I'll go with you," Christina said, resting her arm on Martha's shoulder.

"Okay, we'll meet here at four," Mom said. "Goodness, Christina, you could have left that big coat in the car. Don't you want to go back and leave it now?"

"That's okay. It's not heavy." Christina slung the coat over her arm. "See you later."

We watched them heading up the escalator, then looked at each other.

"What?"

"I don't know," Mom said. "Something about

that child always makes me feel sad."

"Which one?" I asked her.

After an hour of disagreeing about everything I tried on, Mom and I parted company. By three thirty, I'd bought pants on my own and was browsing through Broydan's early spring sportswear. From the corner of my eye, I thought I caught a flash of color—Martha's fuchsia rugby shirt—so I started moving that way between the close, circular racks of bright cottons. When I reached the spot, Martha had disappeared but I stopped for a minute to flip through a group of shirts patterned with muted African designs.

Where had Martha disappeared to? I wondered, already bored with the spring outfits I couldn't afford. Maybe she was in a dressing room, although I knew Martha didn't have enough money for such expensive stuff. I didn't think Christina had any cash, either. Well, maybe she's like Jill, I thought. Jill could spend hours trying on clothes she had no intention of buying even when she did have the money. She just got a kick out of seeing herself in the mirror. Enough about Jill, I thought. Where was Martha?

I stepped into the corridor of fitting rooms and listened. Not a sound at first, then a familiar little giggle. I scanned the space beneath the doors for feet. In the fifth cubicle, there were two pairs of running shoes and a rumpled coat on the floor.

"Hello, women!" I pushed against the door. The magnetic latch released and I was looking at them. Martha seemed startled, flushed, ready to cry out. Why was that? Then I saw that Christina was wearing one of the African blouses, her own shirt half covering it as she pushed her arm into the sleeve.

"What are you doing?" I shut the door behind me. The little room was very close.

"Nothing," Martha squeaked. "Trying on stuff." She was staring at Christina, who looked pale although I could see her mouth setting defiantly. She ignored me.

"What are you doing, Christina?" I whispered again.

"We weren't doing anything—" Martha cried.

"Sh-h-h-h." I was amazingly calm, considering the noise of my pulse pounding in my head. "Martha, are you wearing anything that doesn't belong to you?"

"No." Martha burst into tears and turned into the corner, her head against the mirror.

"You're sure?"

"Yes," she sobbed.

"All right. Here. Take this money and go get a Coke or something. And fix your face before Mom sees you. We have to meet her in a few minutes. Now go."

Even with Martha gone, the space in the cubicle was tight, and I felt a quick rush of dampness across my chest. Christina was just looking at me.

"I can't believe this," I said finally. "I really can't."

"I was just trying on a shirt." All the time Christina was twisting herself out of both shirts, working to get her arms free.

"We both know what you were doing, Christina."

"I don't know what you're talking about." The African print fell to the floor.

A sudden knock on the door startled us. "Can I get you another size?" a clerk asked pleasantly.

"No thanks, but here, take this one." I scooped up the shirt and held it over the door. "She's decided not to get it."

"Oh, all right. If I can be of any help, you let me know," the voice said, drifting away.

"What if you'd been caught? And what about Martha? She's twelve years old, for God's sake." My throat felt parched and I swallowed hard, trying to prevent its closing up.

186

"I wasn't taking it." Christina was buttoning her own shirt now. She slipped into the bulky old coat. "I swear I wasn't."

I was too angry to look at her. "It's time to meet Mom."

"I'm telling the truth, Annie. I know I lied to you that one time about sleepwalking, but that was because I was so embarrassed. I'm telling the truth now, I swear."

We rode all the way to Christina's in silence.

"Everybody's worn out, huh?" Mom said from behind the wheel. "Well, you've got the rest of the weekend to recuperate."

My mind was spinning. The makeup in Martha's room. I'd have to look at it. It was probably expensive—too expensive for Christina. And Martha, what about her? I couldn't believe she'd steal anything, but when we were alone, I'd have to find out for sure.

But my real dilemma was Christina herself. What would I do about her? What *could* I do? It would be my word against hers, and I had no real proof of anything. I turned for a moment to study her shadowy profile. Her face looked hooded, her eyes hidden in thick lashes, half-closed lids. Who is she? I wondered suddenly. What if we don't know

Christina Moore at all?

ஐ

"Please don't tell!" Martha grabbed my arm, pulling me into her room. "Please don't, Annie." The door slammed shut behind us.

"Where's the makeup?" I pulled away from her and started jerking open her dresser drawers. "Where is it?"

Martha pointed to a box in the middle drawer, then put both hands over her face, hiding her tears while I dumped the contents of the box on her bed. Plastic cases of eye shadow and blush, cylinders of mascara and eyeliner, bottles of makeup base, lipsticks, cologne, tubes and tubs of cleansers, removers, masques—all department-store quality. "Three kinds of cologne and all this blush. It's expensive, Martha. What if she stole all this? You've seen this makeup before, haven't you?"

"Yes, but how was I supposed to know how much it costs?" Martha was quivering between tears and anger. "I'm not allowed to wear anything but lipstick. If you're so smart, why didn't you figure it out?"

"I didn't know there was this much of it." I dropped the cosmetics back in the box and sat down on the bed to think. Martha was still sobbing. "The

---

188

sweater! That new sweater she wore to the dance! Where did it come from?"

"I don't know," Martha cried. "I don't know anything."

I softened my tone. "Okay. So just tell me what happened today."

"We were looking at the shirts." Martha blew her nose and came to sit beside me. "And Christina said she thought she'd try one on. She told me to wait there, but I got tired of waiting, so I went in the dressing room. She had the shirt on and she asked me if I liked it. I said I did, and then she started putting her shirt on over it. I didn't know what to say. I mean, I couldn't believe she was really going to take it. I thought she was teasing me or something, so I said for a joke, 'That's really going to buzz,' talking about those alarms at the doors, and she said no it wasn't because the shirt didn't have one of those detector gadgets. She said you'd be surprised how many clothes get skipped over. You just have to look a few minutes to find one. That's when you came in." Martha leaned into my shoulder, wanting to be hugged. "I was so scared, Annie. I didn't know what to do."

"You should have left. If something like this happens to you again, you get out of there fast." I put my arm around her to pull her close. "You were going to tell me, weren't you, Martha?"

"I don't know," she admitted. "She's your friend and everything. And she'd be in such bad trouble."

"But you're my sister. You come first, don't ever forget that." I smoothed her hair back from her forehead and kissed her gently.

"You aren't going to tell Mom and Dad, are you? Please don't, Annie. Nothing bad happened, did it? You don't know that she took the makeup or the sweater. Maybe she wasn't taking the shirt, either. Maybe it just looked like it. Maybe it really was a joke."

"I don't know what to do, honey." Already I was facing the repercussions of exposing Christina. My folks would probably say she couldn't stay here anymore. Would that mean she'd have to drop out of the play? Everybody would want to know the reason, wouldn't they? Mom and Dad would probably insist on talking to her parents. Martha was right. It didn't seem worth it when nothing had really happened. "Don't ever go shopping with her again, no matter what."

"I promise." Martha sighed.

"Some people have a disease like that." I hugged

her hard. "They just can't help taking stuff. That doesn't mean they aren't nice in other ways."

"We're making hot chocolate!" Mom called from the bottom of the stairs.

"Coming!" we called back in unison.

"You're going out with Peter again tonight?" Mom asked when Martha and I had joined the rest of the family in the kitchen.

"Two nights in a row. Sounds serious to me," Dad teased.

I didn't answer. I was remembering the night before, how Peter and I had sat for hours talking in a booth at Giovanni's. It had been quiet there with most of the high school at the basketball game. Then we'd taken a walk along the edge of the lake, although the thermometer reading was in the twenties. The night had been still, the stars brilliant and close, the moonlight catching in the icy snow on the edge of the path. "Silver apples of the moon," Peter had said, touching my cold cheeks.

I couldn't remember what we'd talked about. Nothing really important. And yet now I knew that everything was okay between us.

Greg jiggled the back of my chair to bring me back to the present. "I think they're going steady," he was saying. "Personally, I don't believe in it."

"You don't believe in anything but basketball," Martha said.

"What's happening with you and Amanda, Greg?" Mom asked, and I was glad to have the conversation diverted.

"She's going to chase him until he catches her." Dad was stirring cocoa mix into the heated milk on the stove. "Just like it was with us, sweetheart."

"I never chased you a day in my life," Mom said. "Would anyone like an oatmeal cookie? There're six left."

"I want one with lots of raisins," Martha said. She leaned against the back of my chair, her arms resting over my shoulders.

I squeezed her hand gently. "What are you doing tonight, squirt?" I asked.

"Spending the night with Michelle," Martha said. "Christina picked three songs for us last night, so now we're going to decide which one to do."

"So it's a duet?" Dad brought the mugs of chocolate to the table.

"Yeah, just like Jill and Annie in the sixth grade," Greg said. "Remember that?"

We all laughed, recalling how Jill had gotten the giggles in the middle of the number and I'd had to finish alone. We were pathetic.

"Are things okay with you and Jill?" Mom asked. "I haven't seen her in weeks."

"She's around," I said. "We're all so busy with our own stuff lately."

"Well, tell her we miss her," Mom said.

I wrapped my hand around the hot mug, feeling the burn in my fingertips. I wished straightening out things with Jill could be that easy. I wished I could start talking and tell everybody everything— not just about Christina but about how unsure I was about lots of things, how afraid of being wrong or left out or criticized.

I sipped the hot chocolate. The warmth seemed to slip into my bones, and I shivered a little, feeling its comfort. The debate—that was the next order of business. I'd call the students on both teams tomorrow and arrange a meeting for Monday night. I'd convince them to go ahead with it. I knew I'd have Dan and Phoebe on my side—maybe even Jill because no matter how she protested, she'd enjoy the excitement of it. The rest would fall in line. As much research as we'd already done, we could be ready in no time. We'd put up posters advertising it at school, too. We'd be fearless.

Conversation in the kitchen circled around me, but I didn't hear it. "We're definitely going ahead with the debate," I announced suddenly and more loudly than I'd intended.

"Why, of course you are," Mom said with a smile, and no one offered a rebuttal.

19

Christina stayed over for the Shakespeare meeting. At bedtime when she came back into my room after her shower, I was waiting.

"Martha told me everything," I said.

"About what?" She was carefully folding her clothes at the end of her bed.

"She thinks you were taking the shirt, Christina."

"And you believe a little kid?" she asked. "You know how she loves intrigue." She was smiling, but I knew she could see I wasn't buying it. "Annie, it was just a joke and Martha's too dumb to get it!"

"Martha is not dumb. And she's not a liar, either," I said evenly.

"And you think I am? Well, I'm not!" Christina sat down on the edge of the bed and buried her face in her hands. Her hair was damp from the shower, and curls sprung and danced. "You hate me!" she said softly through her hands. "You've never liked me, Annie, not really. Nobody likes me. The only reason you've ever been nice to me is because you feel sorry for me. Well, don't. I don't need it and I don't want it."

She was right. I had felt sorry for her in the beginning, but not anymore. "What about the makeup?"

"You went through my makeup?" Christina lifted her tear-streaked face long enough to give me a tremulous little smile. "My aunt is the cosmetics buyer for a big department store in Raleigh. She gets free samples and gives them to me." Her voice trembled with disappointment.

"But—" I was remembering that Christina's grandparents didn't approve of makeup.

"She's Daddy's sister," Christina went on, as if she'd anticipated the question. "That side of the family wears makeup, Annie. You should see my aunt's outfits. She gets a discount, of course, but even her blouses cost at least a hundred dollars. She's hoping to come to *Kiss Me, Kate.* Then you'll see." She got up and blew her nose.

I'd planned to ask her about the sweater, but now I wondered what good it would do. She'd already said her dad sent her money, and how could I counter that?

"Your dad's coming to the play, isn't he?" I was watching her through the mirror.

"Of course he is," Christina said. "He comes almost every Sunday. He has a business, and people in business have to stay right there all the time. He's not like college professors, who can be home practically whenever they want to."

"What kind of business?"

"What?" Christina turned around, her hands crossed under her chin as if to ward off cold.

"Your dad's business?" I hated the nagging tone I heard in my voice but I refused to back down.

"Oh, he's—he's in dry cleaning." She twirled back to the dresser and picked up her brush. Her hair lifted against the bristles. "He has a chain of dry cleaners, three in Charlotte and two more in little towns near there. It's a big business."

"And he's trying to sell them and come here and live with his in-laws?" I felt squeamish, like I did when Rosie ripped at the flesh of a quivering rabbit. Suddenly I wanted Christina to have an answer.

"Well, obviously we'll build a house, Annie," she said, impatience edging her voice. "We have the plans and everything. It'll be right next to Grandpa's. Maybe we'll build Grandpa and Grandma a new house, too. A smaller one but really nice. Our house is going to be brick. Two story. Actually, it'll be a lot like this one." She turned down her bed and crawled in, then rolled onto her side, her face hidden under her dark hair.

I switched off the light. The sheets were chilly, and I lay still waiting for the bed to warm around me. She hadn't broken. She hadn't even wavered. I was grateful, too. I guess I didn't really want any evidence against her. It was easier not to know.

"Annie." Christina's voice came suddenly, softly, filling the dark. "You're the best friend I've ever had."

I drifted, lurched back awake, left myself floating again. You're wearing a parachute, I reminded myself, my head already cloudy with sleep. Pull the cord.

ë

"We're going ahead with the debate," I told Ms. Langley after English class on Tuesday. "The teams met last night and decided. We have the Presbyterian Church fellowship hall Sunday afternoon at three."

"I suppose I don't have a prayer of stopping

you," Ms. Langley said. She was gathering papers on her desk.

"No, ma'am."

"Well, you know I can't join you either. Not that I wouldn't like to." Ms. Langley smiled.

"You can be in the audience, can't you?"

"I don't see why not." She rested her hand on my arm. "Are you going to use the format we'd planned?"

"Yes. And don't worry, Ms. Langley. Mom's helping us. Dan's mother, too. And Phoebe's parents are finding judges. We're even having refreshments."

"Well, I've always heard that if students want something done at school, they should tell their mothers." Ms. Langley laughed.

At rehearsal that afternoon, I could hardly concentrate on the music. I kept glancing up at the stage where Peter and Amanda were rehearsing the scene in which they argue about Lilli's leaving the show to marry a senator. I could see Christina in the wings waiting for her next entrance. She gave me a little wave, but the next time I looked, she and Jill were huddled together, whispering. I looked away.

In front of me in the pit, Mr. Dorsey was trying to get our attention for the "I Sing of Love" number; his shoulders squared, he raised his baton and he gave us that "I know you can do it" smile before the first downbeat. Out of the corner of my eye, I could see Christina dancing onto the stage and swinging lightly into the arms of Dan, who had entered from the opposite wing. They swayed together, singing.

Now Peter was in the wings. Since dress rehearsals were still a couple of weeks away, he and Jill and Amanda were getting to watch the number. I could imagine the confusion backstage when dress rehearsals started. Jill had been appointed dresser, since her big number was the first one of the show, so she and Phoebe would be frantically jerking Velcro fasteners, exchanging shirts and dresses, zipping and combing. Thank goodness Phoebe was organized, I thought. I didn't think Jill would ever get it done by herself.

Mr. Dorsey was rapping lightly on my music stand with his baton. I took the note he handed me.

Come to the office immediately, it read. I handed the note back to Mr. Dorsey for him to read. He nodded, so I got up and laid my clarinet across my chair. That was when I saw my hands trembling. They moved on their own as if disconnected, and I could feel my pounding heart and my mouth was dry. Flight or fight, which is it? I wondered.

The breezeway and school corridor were empty. All I could hear were my sneakers squishing slightly on the slick terrazzo floor.

"There you are," the secretary said brightly. "She's waiting for you."

I knocked once and then pushed the door open. Ms. Fletcher was working at her desk, and the afternoon sun rimmed her stiffly arranged hair like a white halo.

"Anne," she said, motioning toward a chair.

I wanted to stand, but I didn't trust my knees so I sat, feeling my chest contract on shallow ragged breaths.

"I've seen the posters announcing the debate," Ms. Fletcher said and waited as if she expected me to explain. When I didn't respond, she went on, "And just now I heard an announcement about it on the radio. On Community Calendar."

Mom strikes again. I held my hands tightly together on my lap.

Ms. Fletcher waited. She seemed to be staring at my flushed cheeks. What did she expect me to say?

"You said not on school time, so it's not on school time," I said, trying to sound confident. "It's on our time. Sunday at three at the Presbyterian Church."

"I heard." Ms. Fletcher sighed heavily. "What is this really about, Anne? I don't believe you people care this much about Shakespeare."

"We tried to tell you." I could feel my voice getting stronger. "It's about intellectual freedom. It's about getting to study issues and making our own decisions."

"Well, you've made quite a decision this time," Ms. Fletcher said.

"Yes, ma'am."

"Then I suppose that's all." When Ms. Fletcher stood up, she blocked the sun so that the room darkened slightly around us.

"Yes, ma'am." I didn't get a good breath until I was halfway down the hall.

❧

"I called the television station, too, and they said they'd try to send a crew out," Mom said that evening. "Kids going to school on Sunday—that's a feature for the evening news if I ever heard one."

"Maybe not," Dad said. "If it bleeds, it leads."

"Well, who *said* this was going to be bloodless?" Mom wanted to know.

❧

After rehearsal on Saturday, I went with Peter to fly Rosie while the air was dry and the thermals warm and constant. Off the fist, the hawk flapped upward, found a current, and floated lazily on it.

"I bet she could ride up there for hours," Peter said. "Look at her." The hawk soared and wheeled against the sky.

"I wish I could do that," I said.

"Yeah." Peter sighed. He took my hand, and we sat down together on a flat dry rock in the field. "Hawks mate for life, you know. For several years Dad watched a pair during mating season until one year only the female came to the nest. She repaired it alone, and then she circled the woods all spring, waiting for the male to come. She did that for years."

"I know. Your dad told me."

"Sorry." Peter was still watching Rosie, who flapped her broad wings several times to catch another thermal.

"I don't mind hearing it again." I hugged his arm.

"Even though they've mated for life, they court every spring. They get the nest ready and then they put on this air show you wouldn't believe. The two of them fly in circles, then they connect their talons and spiral. It's incredible." He stood up, searching the sky. "Maybe this is the year I'll let Rosie go. I've been thinking about it." He sighed as if already bereft of her. "But right now I'd better call her in," he said. He whistled a long shrill cry between his teeth. The bird appeared above us, hovering as if following some prey. Then she glided silently across the field in front of us and plunged to the ground.

"Probably a mouse," Peter said. "I'll get her."

"I'll come, too."

"It'll be messy," Peter warned.

"I think I can handle it. I'm getting to be an expert."

On the way home I told him about Christina and the shirt. "What did your folks say?" Peter wanted to know.

"I didn't tell them."

"Annie, come on. This is major stuff."

"But I don't know for sure she was actually shoplifting."

"That is so lame," Peter protested. "Why are you protecting that girl?"

"I'm not."

"Well, I think you are," Peter said. "What about that arsenal of cosmetics you say she's got?"

"Gifts from her aunt." I sighed. "Let's not talk about her anymore. Remember what happened the last time we talked about Christina?"

"We broke up."

I smiled. "Actually we're still broken up. Technically."

Peter pulled the Jeep between the mews and the house. "Let me get Rosie in and I'll fix that."

I waited impatiently, the tunes from *Kiss Me, Kate* humming in my head. I wanted him to hurry. The final meeting about the debate that evening was going to cut into our time together.

"You want to go steady?" I asked before he could even settle behind the wheel again.

"You're asking me?" He was trying to look serious.

"Read my lips. Will—you—go—steady— with—me?"

A few minutes later, when Peter's dad pulled in behind us and touched his horn to get our attention, we were still kissing. I wasn't one bit embarrassed.

20

By quarter of three the next afternoon, the fellowship hall of the church was half full and we were all pacing nervously around a tiny Sunday School room, muttering our speeches to ourselves.

Mom knocked once and stuck her head in. "It's mostly parents. A bunch from Whitney High, a few university people, and I think I spotted some faculty from the other county schools." She was beaming. "It looks like our advertising worked!"

"Ei-i-i-i," Jill squealed. "I'm so scared!"

"You'll be fine," Christina said to her. "Now let me hear your main point again."

"The writers who didn't accept the man from Stratford as the author of the plays," Jill intoned. "Mark Twain—then I say what he said about it. Charles Dickens—then I say what he said about it.

Ralph Waldo Emerson blah, blah, blah . . . who else?" She frowned and shook her hands anxiously. "Oh, Walt Whitman. Samuel Johnson. Alfred, Lord Tennyson. Oliver Wendell Holmes. And Freud."

"Great." Christina hugged her. "She's got it, guys. We're ready."

"Even Ernie. Right, Ernie?" Phoebe asked.

Ernie was twisting his finger in his shirt collar as if he hoped to stretch it an inch. It was the first time I'd seen him in a tie since our eighth-grade graduation. "Yeah," he mumbled.

"Give us your opening line, Ern," Eric said.

Ernie screwed up his face, puffed out his chest, and said loudly, "William Shaksper of Stratford did not have the education necessary to write the plays and poems attributed to him."

"Whoa," Eric said. "He's got it down!"

The door opened again after a quick knock. "It's almost three," Mom said. "Ready?"

I could feel my stomach knotting. All day my shoulders had felt tight, but now the ache was moving up my neck. "Let's all take a few deep breaths," I said. "And remember, we don't have to prove anything. They do."

"The superintendent is out there," Greg said

over Mom's shoulder. "And the TV people just got here."

"Let's do it, gang!" Eric said, giving Ernie a high sign.

Since Dan was captain of the Stratford team, he introduced their arguments first. I listened intently, half expecting them to have stumbled onto a discovery, but there was nothing new. Dan's strongest argument was the one I'd expected—that in his will, William Shaksper left money to three London actors, two of whom later published the First Folio of Shakespeare's plays.

Then it was our turn. During the past three days, I had practiced my opening argument so many times I could say it in my sleep, but now, facing a real audience, I found myself listening to my own voice as if I'd never heard it before. I could hear the effectiveness of the phrases Peter had told me to punch, the pauses he'd recommended. I sounded confident.

The judges were in the front row—Harry Jenkins from the newspaper, who was giving up the second half of the Wake Forest game to be there; a woman I'd never seen before, who had to be the university lawyer; and the director of the community theater. They all had poker faces, so I looked slightly above their heads like Peter had told me. He was in the back row, but I didn't want to look at him, either. Just thinking about him could give me a catch in my throat. I concentrated on what I was saying, amazed at how well my argument countered Dan's opening speech. I almost wished I could elaborate on each point—Mom's voice kept trying to pop into my head but I pushed it away. Elaboration was the job of my teammates.

"We do not accept the premise that genius springs from nowhere. A vocabulary of fifteen thousand words, knowledge of foreign lands and languages, of court life and law, requires a life of study and of intense involvement in the world," I said carefully, trying not to sprint to the end. "We submit that, based on the authenticated information known about William Shaksper of Stratford, there is reasonable doubt that he could be the author of the plays and poems attributed to him. Thank you."

A scattering applause startled me and I tried not to smile. After returning to my seat I glanced back at Peter. He winked. I had done okay.

Randy on the Stratford team was speaking about Shakespeare's childhood and education, but I could hardly listen. The judges down the row from me each had legal pads, and the theater director, a young man wearing black except for bright-red socks, was scribbling. Harry Jenkins, his blank pad on the floor at his feet, looked decidedly bored, but the lawyer, her glasses pushed up onto her head, seemed to be absorbing every word. There was no way to tell how it was going.

The Stratford proponent ended with "We contend that William Shakespeare attended the guild school in Stratford, where he was taught by graduates of Oxford and Cambridge universities. His education there would be the equivalent of our college education."

Then it was Ernie's turn. He cleared his throat and took a sip of water just like Mom had told him to. His voice cracked a little starting, but then I could actually see him gaining confidence as he talked. He ended his argument by quoting two lines from the Stratford man's tombstone: "'Blessed be the man that spares these stones, And cursed be he that moves my bones.' Are we to believe," he went on heartily, "that the same man who composed such doggerel also wrote these words of Henry the Fifth, spoken to his soldiers before the Battle of Agincourt: 'From this day to the ending of the world, But we in it shall be remembered—We few, we happy few, we band of brothers; For he today that sheds his blood with me Shall be my brother.'"

He sat down, his cheeks and neck suddenly flushed. He rolled his notes into a cylinder, flattened them again, repeated the process. I watched the rattling paper, wondering what the judges were thinking. So far, so good, right? Both sides were really prepared. Everybody was serious. It couldn't be going better, and yet I felt clammy and my heart was racing. We still had Jill's turn to get through—after Ernie, she was the one on our team most likely to panic. I glanced behind me again. The superintendent of schools was there, and Ms. Langley was down the row from him. Maybe this was a big mistake. I looked down at my list, which had somehow gotten crumpled in my hand. Jill next, then Eric, Christina, and finally Phoebe who had the stickiest point to make. I flattened the paper on my lap, wishing the whole ordeal were over.

Finally Phoebe was at the lectern countering the proposed dates of the plays, which had been assigned on the assumption that the man from Stratford had written them. Her argument was that the plays were not the work of a young man but of a person of experience and maturity. "An example of such a man would be Edward de Vere, the Seventeenth Earl of Oxford, who remains the most likely candidate for authorship."

We had spent half of a planning session arguing about including that sentence. The idea, Phoebe kept saying, was to cast doubt about the Stratford man, not propose someone else.

"But I think mentioning De Vere strengthens our argument," Christina had put in. "Hearing about him helped convince me."

"Me, too," Jill said. "Like if we say Shakespeare didn't write the plays, the next question is, well then who did?"

The guys hadn't seen a problem either way, so Phoebe and I gave in and the reference to De Vere stayed.

Before I knew it, Dan was up listing the Stratford points for the last time and it was my turn again. I reiterated my team's arguments quickly and then took my final minute to quote from *Hamlet*. I'd practiced this most of all. Standing in front of my mirror, I'd seen my mouth quiver with the words, a man's plea that his life and work someday be acknowledged. I can't do it, I'd cried to Peter, stopping and starting for the umpteenth time. Now I suddenly felt calm. An unexpected confidence opened my chest and I breathed deeply before quoting from Hamlet's death scene: "'If thou didst ever hold me in thy heart, Absent thee from felicity awhile, And in this harsh world draw thy breath in pain, To tell my story. . . .'"

It was over. The minister, Mr. Carlyle, stood up to say that the judges' decision would be announced momentarily.

"Aw man, they didn't even look awake," Ernie whispered beside me.

"It's okay." I was too tired to think. "At least we did it."

Christina leaned over my shoulder. "You were great. That bit from *Hamlet* was terrific. I thought I'd cry myself."

Mr. Carlyle was collecting a card from each judge, and he returned to the lectern with them. "Before I announce the results, I would like to say that I consider all the students who participated in this event, and even the audience here today, winners. I for one didn't know anything about this issue but now I feel enlightened. I congratulate both teams on their hard work. It's wonderful to see young people with such enthusiasm for new ideas." There was a small burst of applause.

"Now as you recall, the proposition for this debate is 'Resolved: That William Shakespeare of

Stratford is the author of the poems and plays attributed to him.' Therefore, a yes vote will constitute a vote for the Stratford team and a no vote will be a vote for the anti-Stratford team." He studied the cards for a moment. "The decision of the judges is one yes vote and two no votes, so the anti-Stratford group wins."

When the applause died down again, Mom went to the lectern and thanked the judges for participating and the audience for attending. "Please join us for refreshments," she said. She and some of the other mothers had spent part of Saturday making finger sandwiches and cookies. Dan's mother was already at the punch bowl ready to serve.

In one corner of the room, the university lawyer was in front of the TV camera crew's bright light, a microphone held to her mouth by an eager young reporter I recognized from the evening news.

"You and Dan get over there. This is your show." Mom practically pushed us in that direction.

I felt too tired to move or think, but I forced myself to listen to the lawyer while Dan and I waited our turn. "I believe that the students opposing the Stratford position presented better organized and more convincing arguments," she said. "As I'm sure you know, the criterion for debate is not the truth or falsity of the issue but the presentation of the arguments. 'Did the opposing team refute the arguments?' is the question the judges must respond to. Both teams did very well and are to be congratulated for their preparation on such an interesting and complicated issue."

Drawn in front of the camera, I felt suddenly energized again. "How did this event get started?" the reporter wanted to know.

"It began with our class's interest in the true identity of Shakespeare," I said before Dan could answer. "We planned to have this debate in our classroom, but when it was canceled, we were still interested in the question, so we decided to do it anyway." Don't embarrass the school, Mom and Dad had said. Don't accuse anybody of anything. "We appreciate the Presbyterian Church letting us use their space, and the minister, Mr. Carlyle, for serving as moderator, don't we, Dan?"

"We sure do," Dan said just before the reporter took the mike away and faced the camera himself. "And so education continues through the weekend at Whitney High," he said. "People who complain about our young people should have come out today to hear these Whitney High School students. The school and the community can only be proud of their enthusiasm as well as their academic achievements."

Peter was there, pulling me into the hall where he hugged me hard. "You were great," he said. "Did you see Ms. Langley in the audience? She just ducked out, but she said to tell you she's proud of all of you."

"I'm just glad it's over," I said, collapsing against his shoulder. "Bucking authority wears me out."

"Let's take a walk," Peter suggested.

"I can't leave yet. We have to put all the chairs back and clean up the kitchen. Anyway, I want to meet Christina's dad."

"Aw, Christina again," Peter moaned. "'A plague o' both your houses.'"

"Don't say that." I laughed. "It might be true!"

Christina was near the refreshment table when I found her. "So where's your dad?"

"Oh, he couldn't come," Christina said sadly. "He's so disappointed. He called last night and said there was a problem at one of the cleaners. A machine quit or something."

"But your mom's here, right?" I took the cup of punch she handed me. "And your grandparents? I want to meet them."

"They're over there," Christina said, motioning

to a couple talking to Dad. They had gray hair and less than stylish clothes, but they looked younger than I'd expected.

28

After dinner that evening, I found Dad in his study. "What's up, kid?" he asked, closing his book and folding his glasses on his desk. "You ought to hit the sack early tonight. I know you're beat."

"Yeah." I sat across his lap, my head on his shoulder. "It went okay, though, didn't it, Daddy?"

"Sure it went okay. Your side won, didn't it?" He hugged me closer.

"I don't mean that. I mean, we were right to do it, weren't we? I sort of dread school tomorrow."

"Well, don't. I know I played the devil's advocate in this, Annie. I don't want you parroting your mother, you know, taking on her battles and all. I want you to be your own person, and I think you are." He kissed my forehead. "I'm very proud of you."

"Thanks, Dad. Hey, I saw you talking to Christina's grandparents."

He nodded. "Seemed a little shy about being there, but they're nice folks. They appreciate all the time we've been taking with Christina."

"Oh, they said that?" I was looking at the lamplight reflecting on his glasses on the desk. "Dad, they weren't wearing glasses, were they?"

"Well no, I don't think so. Why?"

"Oh, nothing." I nestled more deeply in his arms, but I was remembering how Christina had said her grandparents couldn't drive at night. How could that be if they didn't even need glasses? "I guess I'll do some homework until the eleven o'clock news."

"That's right, you're going to be on TV." He chuckled. "I wonder if Alice Fletcher and Carl Johnson will watch it."

"And what will they think if they do? Now I know why people don't get involved with issues even when they have strong feelings about them."

"It takes courage to change the world. No doubt about that," Dad said. "But now there's just the musical on your agenda, right? I don't suppose there can be a crisis there."

"Not unless Peter gets laryngitis," I said.

All day Monday I expected to get called to the office, but nothing happened. By Tuesday, the buzz about the television coverage of the debate seemed to be over, and I felt a weary kind of relief. We took our final *Julius Caesar* test, too.

"Now we can get on to Milton," Ms. Langley said with a smile. "Milton was truly a scholar, although he knew only eight thousand words as compared to Shakespeare's fifteen thousand."

The class answered with a chorus of moans.

"At least there's no question of who Milton was," she went on undaunted.

"Well, I'll buy that," Ernie said loudly, and we all laughed.

ھ

At rehearsal that afternoon, Christina sang "Always True to You in My Fashion," then the two gunmen rehearsed "Brush up Your Shakespeare" while the orchestra limped along with Mr. Dorsey struggling to direct the singers and the musicians simultaneously. When we finally got a break, I found Peter backstage.

"Where's Jill?" I asked, taking a swallow of his Coke.

"She went to get her driver's license." Christina passed us without stopping.

"Oh good grief, today's her birthday! How could I forget that? I've seen her ten times today and I didn't say a word about it. I haven't gotten her anything, either. Peter, what am I going to do?"

"I'll take you to get something after rehearsal,"

Peter said. "And don't get so worked up, Annie. You've had a lot on your mind."

"Well, I've got to do something about it. Maybe we can all go out for dinner. How about that?"

"It's fine with me," Peter said, "but shouldn't you check with Jill before you start making plans? I mean, maybe she's already doing something."

"I'd know about it! I always get invited." But suddenly I wasn't so sure. But we're still best friends, I thought, pushing aside my apprehension. Nothing can change that.

Ms. Dalton was calling us to our places. "Tell Jill I need to talk to her when she gets back," I said to Peter before hurrying out front to the pit.

Rehearsal ended and Jill still hadn't shown up. Peter gave Christina and me a ride home.

"I just don't understand where she could be," I said.

"Maybe there was a line at the examiner's office today," Peter said.

Christina didn't say anything.

"Can you take me to get her something now?" I asked him. "Want to come, Christina?"

Greg's car was in the drive beside Mom's.

"I'll stay here," Christina said. "Greg and I have a French test tomorrow."

"Tell Mom I'll be home soon." I handed Christina my house key at the curb. "And if Jill calls, tell her I'll call back."

But an hour later when Peter dropped me off at home, Christina had already left. "Did her mom come early?" I asked in the kitchen.

"It wasn't her mom," Greg said from his usual place in front of the open refrigerator. "Jill picked her up."

21

The next morning Peter and I were sitting in his Jeep in the commuter lot at school.

"So Jill wasn't home when you went over," Peter said. "What's the big deal?"

"Her mom didn't say where she was—that's the big deal. In fact, she seemed a little embarrassed, like she didn't know exactly what to say. Finally she told me they hadn't planned anything special for Jill's birthday because she wants to take a bunch of us to the beach in the spring for a big weekend party."

"An excellent idea."

"So I just left the gift and went home." The heater was finally blowing its thin warmth against my legs, and I leaned toward it. "I think her mom knows we've had a falling out."

"Oh, is that what you call it?"

"I guess."

"I don't understand why you two can't just get over it. We did." He touched the back of his hand against my cheek.

"It's women's stuff," I said.

"Which makes it more complicated than problems with guys?"

"Sometimes."

"Maybe you're both too stubborn." His fingers found the tight cords in my neck and squeezed gently.

I shivered. "Ah-h-h, that's wonderful. Keep doing that. What I really need is a massage."

"This weekend. Now that hunting season's over, I've got plenty of time for good stuff like back rubs. Rosie's already beginning to molt."

"I wish I could molt," I said. "I'd like an excuse to stay in for a few weeks."

Peter laughed. "You losing feathers? I can't imagine it. Anyway, remember when you had mono? You just about drove me crazy. Jill, too."

I frowned, remembering I hadn't finished telling him about Jill. "Yesterday while we were out getting her present, she came over in her new car, picked up Christina, and took her home. At least, I guess she did. Christina didn't come back."

"Her new car?"

"A white Honda Prelude. The point is, Christina got the first ride." Christina's bus was pulling past us. "Maybe I should tell Jill about that day in the mall. What do you think? Would I be telling her just because she and Christina are friends? I mean, am I jealous?"

"I don't know. Are you?"

"A little bit, but I don't want to be. I wanted Jill and Christina to like each other. I wanted all of us to like each other."

"Yeah, Annie's perfect little world," Peter said. "Let me know when you get it."

"So what should I do?"

"To quote the Bard, 'To thine own self be true,'" Peter said.

"According to Mom, Polonius meant look out for number one."

"Exactly." Peter leaned over and kissed my cheek. "I think that's what Christina does, Annie. I think that's what she's always done."

❧

The usual crowd was eating together in the cafeteria but today Christina joined us with her container of cottage cheese and carrot sticks.

"No wonder you're so skinny," Phoebe said. "Here, have some pizza. It'll be vegetarian if you take the pepperoni off. You need some bread, woman."

Christina took a small wedge and carefully picked off the greasy curls of meat.

"I wish I could be thin once in my life, but I hate stuff like that," Jill moaned, eyeing Christina's lunch. "Cottage cheese tastes like wet chalk."

"If you go on a diet, you'll have to give up all those Snickers," Peter said.

"I know." Jill rolled her eyes toward the ceiling. "Imagine life without chocolate. I mean, would it be worth living?"

"No!" we chorused.

"A lot of people eat all they want and then throw up," Christina said.

"That's so sick," Dan said. "Jill, don't you try that."

"Are you kidding? Stick my finger down my throat? Gross!" Jill said.

"There're lots of ways to make yourself throw up," Christina said. "I've read about it."

"Well, don't tell us," I said. "I'm trying to eat this pizza."

"Yeah, Christina," Dan said. "Don't give her any

ideas. Jill here will try almost anything."

"Dan Coleman, don't tell them that!" Jill groaned and hugged his arm. "It's not true!"

But I knew Dan was right. Jill could be talked into anything. So I'd talk to her. I'd tell her about Christina outside Greg's door, maybe even about the shoplifting. I'd even apologize to her if I had to, although I still thought she was wrong to sympathize with Peter instead of with me. But it would be worth it to make everything okay between us again.

&

That afternoon during the first rehearsal break and before I could lose my nerve, I went backstage to the dressing room. Jill was alone.

"Hi, I need to talk to you," I said as brightly as I could manage.

"About what?" She already sounded impatient. "I'm busy here, Annie. I've got all these costumes to get organized."

"Why are you acting like this?" I was trying to stay calm, but I could feel my voice rising over the noise of hangers scraping the racks. Maybe this was a lousy idea, but there was no backing out now.

"Acting like what? I'm not acting at all," Jill said. "You're the dramatic one. You're the one who always has to be right about everything."

"That's not true, Jill!"

"Oh, yes it is." Jill stopped straightening the clothes but hung on to the metal rack, her arms stretched over her head. "You want to be right all the time, Annie, but other people have opinions, too, you know. Other people have feelings."

"I don't know what you're talking about. We had an argument—about loyalty, that's all it was."

"Hardly," Jill said. "And speaking of loyalty, I know you talked to Christina about me—like about drivers' ed. and Dan and—well, personal stuff."

"I did not!" I started, but I was already remembering a time when I did. "Listen, Jill, I just want things to be like they used to be. Before Christina."

"So now Christina's to blame?" Jill asked.

"I'm not blaming her," I said wearily, "but she's here, she's part of all of this, isn't she?"

"And whose idea was that? You wanted me to like her, right? You wanted everything your way. Well, now you've got it. I like Christina fine, I really do. She's fun and she wants to do things. She's not a stick-in-the-mud like some people I know, and she doesn't go around making accusations, either." Jill's face was flushed. "In fact, we all think she's a wonderful addition to our crowd—so thank you very much, Annie."

The orchestra was tuning up. "I've got to go," I said.

"Yeah, well, I'm busy myself." Dust flew off a velvet cape that Jill was shaking.

I turned away.

"Oh, thanks for the tape yesterday," Jill called after me, and I thought I heard a tinge of regret in her voice. I turned back to it but she had disappeared and there was just the sound of swishing satin and the orchestra's sour A note floating in the dusty air.

I waited until bedtime to knock on Greg's door. "Yeah?" he answered.

"Got a minute?" I asked, letting myself in. He was at his desk, where Dad's old drafting lamp formed a circle of white light on his history book. "Oh, you're studying."

"And I'll take any excuse to stop," he said, swinging his chair around. Bono was singing a track from the *Rattle and Hum* tape, but Greg turned it down.

I sat down on the edge of his bed. "I know you don't like Christina," I began.

Greg waited. "So?"

"So. Sometimes I don't think I like her either."

"What's this all about, Annie?"

I hoped for a burst of courage like the one that had gotten me to his door in the first place, but none came. "Why did you dance with Christina that time?"

"Because she asked me! I was just standing there with the guys waiting for Amanda in the john and she came right up and asked me. I couldn't embarrass her by saying no. Jeez, you and Mom would have had a fit." He stretched, then folded his arms behind his head. "So I figured, what the heck, the kid's got a crush on me. The least I can do is dance with her for two minutes."

"You know she stayed over that night," I said uneasily. "And Greg, I found her outside your room in the middle of the night. She said she was just going to talk to you and I tried to believe her—I mean, her own brother died and all—but now I don't know."

"Aw, man, that's all I need—that girl accusing me of something."

"Anyway, nothing happened," I said. "You see, in a way that's the real problem—nothing ever really happens."

"Hi, what's going on?" Mom was in the doorway.

"Just talking," Greg said.

"Well good night, kiddos." She pulled the door shut.

"Aren't you going to tell her?" Greg wanted to know.

I shook my head. "Maybe I should have weeks ago, but it's too late now. Anyway, the whole business sounds so stupid. I mean, people don't act like this."

"Maybe some of them do, Annie." Greg was making circles on the margin of his notebook.

"Well, I did try to tell Jill, but she wouldn't listen." I sighed. "And last night when I went over to give her a birthday present, her mom seemed uncomfortable, like there was something I shouldn't know. I think Jill and Christina were out together."

"Maybe they deserve each other," Greg said. "Anyway, you're not responsible for everything that happens, Annie. Just do your own thing and don't think so much."

I got up and pressed my hands on his shoulders. "Great advice," I said but back in my room, I felt my resolve softening in a flood of loneliness, and I had to force myself not to punch Jill's number.

❧

"I called Danice Moore and invited her to stay

for dinner tonight," Mom told me in the kitchen Thursday afternoon. "She said she couldn't stay."

Dad folded the sports section at the table and took off his glasses. "Carolina's in the hole again. Sometimes those guys can't buy a basket. So how's the play going, Annie?"

"Okay." I shrugged. "Actually it's pretty ragged. We're having the technical run-through Saturday. Ms. Dalton warned us it would take all day, too."

"Well, the show's the thing," Dad said. "Where's Christina, anyway?"

At that moment we heard Christina at the piano in the living room and Martha's voice lifting over the music.

Mom said, "Ms. Moore couldn't come for dinner because she has a date."

I had to look at her to be sure I'd heard correctly. "But—"

Mom raised her eyebrows and nodded toward the living room, reminding me to whisper.

"What's going on?" Dad asked.

"According to Christina, her dad is in Charlotte selling his business so he can move here with them," I explained softly.

"Well, maybe she didn't mean a date," Dad said. "Maybe she meant an engagement, like a business dinner or something."

"She said date, Larry, and she meant date. I know what I heard." Mom was emphatic.

"Well, maybe they're separated and Christina doesn't want to talk about it," Dad suggested.

"And maybe," I said with a sigh, "Christina doesn't have a father at all."

22

"This is never going to end," Peter said when we were breaking for lunch on Saturday. All morning we'd limped through the technical rehearsal, stopping for every light cue and sound check. So far the orchestra hadn't completed one uninterrupted number, the prop telephone had fallen off the wall, Amanda's dressing-room screen had been knocked over, and the tech crew couldn't decide on the length of a fadeout.

"It has to get better. This is just the dark before the dawn," I said. We grabbed our bag lunches and headed for the back of the theater.

"I don't see why we can't go to Burger King," Jill complained, coming up the aisle behind us.

"Because we'd never come back." Dan grabbed her around the waist as he passed. "I'll go get sodas.

Be back in two shakes."

"No eating in the theater!" Ms. Dalton called just when we'd settled on the last rows. "You have three choices—the T.A. room, the band room, or under the breezeway."

"But it's twenty degrees out there," Christina said. "Let's sit in your car, Jill. We can turn on the heater and the radio."

"You two go ahead if you want to asphyxiate yourselves," I said.

"Give us a break, Annie." Jill shrugged. "All this doom and gloom all the time."

"The T.A. room," Peter said, leading the way. He caught my hand, pulling me along after him. "Don't make a scene, Annie. It's not worth it."

"The rest of you get plenty of chances." I leaned into his arm. "And I bet it would make me feel a lot better."

"Temporarily." Peter glanced over his shoulder to make sure Christina and Jill, who were following us, weren't within hearing. "Then you'll start feeling bad about it." He pushed open the door. "And here's my blushing bride, my Kate!"

Amanda was leaning back in a chair, her legs resting on another seat. "And I came in here to get some peace," she moaned.

"Like we care," Jill said, pulling the chair from under her legs.

"They're letting us die out there," Christina said, sitting next to Amanda. "The fadeout at the end of my song lasted twenty seconds. I counted them! Twenty! And there I am holding that stupid pose!" She dug into her bag and came up with two tangerines, one of which she held out to Amanda.

"Thanks." Amanda pulled herself erect and began peeling the tangerine. "You sounded great this morning."

"You too." Christina gave her one of those brilliant smiles.

"Well, what about me?" Jill asked, biting into her roast beef sandwich.

"And me?" Peter added.

"Jeez, we're all wonderful!" Dan said, popping his Mountain Dew can.

"Ten more minutes!" Phoebe was in and out before anyone could answer.

"She loves telling us what to do," Amanda complained, catching juice on her chin. "I'm sick of it."

"And you're planning to major in theater?" Peter said. "Get used to it."

"Oh, you'll be wonderful, Amanda!" Christina said.

"In college, it takes at least a year of acting classes just to get onstage," Peter said.

"Not Amanda," Christina said. "She'll be great. Greg thinks so too, Amanda. He was saying just the other day how terrific you are."

"He did?"

I glanced at Peter. Where did this come from? Greg had hardly been home all week.

"Okay, gang!" Ms. Dalton called from the doorway. "Let's get this show back on the road!"

"If such a thing is possible," Peter said, pulling me up and into his arms.

The first half of Scene Five went smoothly until Amanda didn't get her offstage shrieking cue on time. "Maybe we should give it to sound. What do you think, guys?" Ms. Dalton yelled up to the booth. "Before you leave today, get Amanda shrieking on tape."

Then the spotlight on the balcony was two feet off the mark. "I can't play this in the dark!" Amanda called irritably. "I mean, what's the point?"

"All right, cast, let's keep our opinions to ourselves," Ms. Dalton said. "Remember, this is a technical rehearsal—this is where we stay with it till we get the cues right. Guys, set the light on the door and leave it there. Okay, Amanda, make your entrance.

Good! That'll work!"

The first act finally ended with Peter throwing Amanda over his shoulder and carrying her offstage.

"Fifteen-minute break!" Ms. Dalton called as Amanda and Peter came back into the light. Amanda was rubbing her backside. "You really hit me, Peter," she pouted.

"Well, you gave me some belly punches, too," Peter said. "I think I've got a ruptured spleen."

"A little lovers' quarrel?" Christina nudged past me in the aisle.

Randy Dail, who'd been following Christina, stopped beside me. "Wanta get a soda?"

"Sure." I knew he must want something besides a Coke, but what?

We met Christina on her way back to the stage. She was carrying a bottle of mineral water. "For Amanda and me," she said.

"I'm thinking about asking Christina to go to the cast party," Randy said while we waited for the cans to drop through the slot. "What do you think?"

"You might as well. You'll both be there anyway."

Randy handed me the can with an embarrassed

grin. "I guess I'm asking if you think she likes me," he said. "I know this sounds weird but I can't tell. Sometimes she acts like she does and then the next time—"

"She likes you just fine," I said easily. "I'm sure of it." Of course, I didn't know if it was true or not. Maybe with Christina nobody could tell.

I stood under the breezeway after Randy went back inside. I was freezing but I wasn't ready to join the fray. I was thinking about Christina.

A father with five dry-cleaning shops, but where was he? And why wasn't there money for nice clothes? What about a picture of the boyfriend? Wouldn't she have shown me one? And that dilapidated farmhouse where she lived, what about that? And her grandparents? They looked perfectly capable of driving her home from rehearsals. What did it all add up to? A habitual liar? Or a girl so desperate for friends she'd risk anything, do anything? Or was everything she'd told me true?

She wants to be part of things, I thought. Why should I resent that? I should be glad she's making other friends—I was glad. Anyway, after the play, everything would get back to normal. I tossed the empty can into the recycling bin beside the machine.

So much had happened to Christina—she'd lost her brother, she'd moved to a new town and a new school. I couldn't imagine coping with all that. I've never had to do anything hard, I thought suddenly. I've never had a real problem in my life.

I could hear the orchestra tuning. Act Two was bound to go faster, and then there was the rest of the weekend to look forward to.

It was almost five when the final curtain came down. I quickly pulled a drying cloth through my clarinet and put it away.

"Ready?" Peter was at my shoulder.

"Yeah. Maybe we need to give Christina a ride home, though."

"That's one way to keep her from hogging our evening," Peter agreed. Christina was passing. "Need a lift?" he asked her.

"No thanks. I'm going with Amanda," she said without stopping.

"How about that?" Peter whispered. "I just wonder how long it will last."

At least she's not going with Jill, I thought. So why did I still feel left out?

❧

"Go with me to take Clancy for a walk," Mom said on Sunday afternoon. We bundled up in jackets and scarves, knitted hats and gloves while Clancy pawed at the back door, happy to have his leash on.

The sky was overcast and the air felt damp. "Looks like a little snow on the way," Mom said on the sidewalk. "Probably the last blast of winter."

We turned down the street. "Oh, I can hardly wait till spring," I said.

"That's youth for you." Clancy was pulling Mom ahead.

"I just want this play over with. I want everything back like it used to be."

"Well, good luck. One thing I've learned is that everything changes," Mom said. "I used to think I could get my life in order and it would stay that way, but it doesn't happen."

"I hate change."

"Things still aren't okay with you and Jill, are they?" We stopped at a stop sign to let traffic pass.

"Not exactly."

Mom sighed. "Then you ought to do something about it, Annie. I think about my school friends— they were the best friends I've ever had. I don't see them anymore, but I have such wonderful memories. It's hard to have friends like that once you're grown. You get involved with work and family and you end up knowing a lot of people casually, but there's nobody you can talk to all night long like when you were a kid. There's nobody who knows everything about you."

"Not even Dad?"

"Oh, he's my best friend now and I'm glad about that." Mom was getting breathless in the cold air. "But it's not the same as being close to another woman. I wish I had both."

"Jill and Christina are getting to be friends."

"I suspected as much. Christina has a way about her."

There it was again—a cool, curling feeling in my gut that made me want to twist away.

"Let me run with him awhile." I took Clancy's leash from her. "I'll see you back at the house."

"Well, cover your mouth with your scarf!" Mom called after me, but I pretended not to hear.

&

Costumes made the difference. What had, from my perspective in the pit, looked ragtag at best became, at the dress rehearsal, infused with color and light. The platforms we'd built seemed more solid, our corners more square, the painted flats more detailed. And the voices embodied in satin and velvet became impressively assured. The dancers, too, seemed confident. They smiled broadly, risking the confinements of stage space in their turns. The lifts they'd stumbled through for two months suddenly seemed winged.

Dressed in costumes designed to look like ordinary rehearsal clothes for the opening scene, Christina and Dan really did look like two young hoofers in their first big show. Amanda and Peter in their elegant dressing gowns became sophisticated, world-wise performers, and their verbal sparring had a new snap to it.

"Great first act," I said to Peter during the intermission break. "And I love the tights."

He blushed under his heavy makeup. "Yeah well, there's been a lot of grousing backstage about them. I don't know how these guys thought they were going to play Shakespeare without tights."

"They thought they were playing Cole Porter." I handed him a cup of water and watched him guzzle it. Water dripped off his chin and made narrow tracks in the makeup on his neck.

"Hey, you'll be too waterlogged to sing a note." I took the cup back and glanced at my watch. "It's already quarter to five. We'll be here past dinnertime."

"I've got the Jeep. I'll drive you home—you and Christina, unless, of course, she's going with Jill. Or Amanda," Peter teased.

"She's coming with us," I said. "Five more nights—count 'em."

I held up my fingers, but he took my hand instead, curling my fingers into his palm. "We hope," he said.

&

When Peter dropped us off, Ms. Moore's car was in front of the house. "Oh no," Christina groaned. "I told her I'd call her when we were finished. I hope she hasn't been a bother."

"Why should she be?"

Christina shrugged, then huddled next to me while I turned the key in the front door. Inside there was a fire in the living-room fireplace, and Mom and Ms. Moore were on the sofa drinking tea.

"Here they are," Mom said.

"Yes, well, thanks for the tea," Ms. Moore said, getting up. She looked tired, her face sallow above the white uniform she was wearing. "Let's go, Christina." She put her arm around her daughter, but Christina stood rigid in her coat, her books tight in her arms.

"Thanks for having her the rest of the week," Ms. Moore said to Mom. "It would be hard to come into town every night."

"We're glad to have her, aren't we?" Mom put her arm around me, and I leaned against her for a moment, smelling the familiar scent of her cologne. It was the White Linen I'd given her for Christmas. "Sure. No problem."

When they were gone, Mom sat back down on the sofa and stared at the fire.

"Aren't we having dinner?" I asked. "I'm starving."

"Pizza. I just called, so it'll be thirty minutes or so." She sounded tired. "Annie, I need to talk to you a minute."

"What is it?" I dropped my jacket in a chair and went to sit beside her.

"Well, I asked Danice Moore which night Christina's father was coming to see the play because we'd like to meet him. She was really embarrassed that Christina hadn't told us they're divorced. She said he hasn't made child support payments in years. She doesn't even know where he is anymore."

"But Christina said—"

"Well, it just isn't true, honey. They moved in with Ms. Moore's parents because they couldn't afford their rent in Charlotte. Everything's gotten so high over the past few years. One-parent families can hardly make it these days. Christina even had to give up her piano lessons."

"But why didn't she just tell us they were divorced? I mean, in a way it would make us more sympathetic with her."

Now's the time, I was thinking. I can tell her everything now.

But Mom went on, "Well, maybe she thinks she was the cause of their splitting up. You know that happens." She squeezed my hand. "Kids think the world revolves around them, and so if anything goes wrong, they just assume responsibility when it really isn't theirs. I'm sure she's heartbroken, poor thing. I'm just telling you so you won't ask her about him anymore."

&

"I just want her out of my life," I said to Peter that night on the phone. "Of course, Mom's oozing sympathy and expects me to do the same."

"I still think you ought to tell your folks all the other stuff that's happened," Peter said.

"How can I now? It'll look like I've decided it's time to 'get Christina.'" I turned on my side, the receiver pressed to my pillow. "Besides, I do feel a little guilty, Peter. I mean, I have everything."

"And you've shared with her plenty," Peter said.

"Mom said I shouldn't say anything to her about her dad, but I want to. I really want to accuse her of lying. Isn't that nasty? Peter, I don't like feeling this way about another person."

"'My tongue will tell the anger of my heart; Or else my heart, concealing it, will break,'" he said in his best dramatic voice.

"Edward de Vere strikes again." I couldn't help but laugh.

"He's got a word for every occasion," Peter said. "'But, soft! what light through yonder window breaks? It is the east, and Juliet is the sun!'"

"Well, this Juliet is fading fast." I snuggled deeper under the covers. There was nothing to do about Christina anyway. "See you tomorrow, Romeo."

"Night, Annie."

"You're a sweetheart, you know that?"

"I love you, too," he said lightly. It was the first time he'd said it, but he hung up before I could answer.

23

Opening night went off without a hitch. One down and three to go, I thought as I hurried backstage after the final curtain. Within minutes, the dressing room was a mob scene. Bouquets of flowers covered the makeup tables, clothes were trampled, costumes were smeared with runny makeup and soft drinks. Phoebe and Jill were frantically rescuing clothes and shoes.

I could help, I thought, but why should I? Jill would probably accuse me of trying to take over. Anyway, I'd done my part. The orchestra had played as if we actually knew the music, and we'd gotten as much applause as anyone onstage.

I leaned against the wall, out of the fray, knowing Peter wouldn't be in a hurry to get showered and changed.

"Hello, Anne." It was Ms. Fletcher, looking starched and sprayed beside me.

I'd been avoiding her since the debate, but there was no escaping this time. "Hi." I straightened my back against the wall, trying not to freak.

"It was a lovely show, so full of energy," she went on. "And quite an audience, too. Hopefully there'll be a full house every night."

"Yes, ma'am."

"I know quite a lot of work went into this." She touched my shoulder lightly. I forced myself not to cringe. "I appreciate any occasion when students band together for a common cause, Anne. There's always something to learn from that kind of experience."

"Yes, ma'am."

"Well, I won't try to push my way through this crowd to speak to the cast. I think a note on the bulletin board tomorrow will have to do."

"I could tell them you were here."

"Thank you."

So she wasn't upset with me, at least not anymore. Mom was right. Sometimes it was easier to get forgiveness than permission.

"I guess Amanda's in here somewhere," Greg said at my shoulder.

"Center stage. See?" I pointed to a flash of red hair in the middle of the room.

"Well, tell her I'll be in Giovanni's."

"Greg, you ought to congratulate her here. It won't mean as much hours from now." Mom had seen to it that he sent flowers, and now I was having to talk him into basic politeness. "What you know about women isn't worth five cents," I said, giving him a little shove into the crowd. He shouldered his way center, and I watched arms go up around his neck, reaching, tugging his head down toward hers. They turned a little, off balance in the tight space. It was Christina who was hugging him.

❧

Our teachers didn't let up on homework all week although we were barely awake in class. Every night Christina and I came home from the show too wired to study or sleep. We would make hot drinks and then search the freezer for goodies Mom had stashed for one of her sugar attacks. She and Dad had seen the show on opening night and had tickets for the closing, too.

Late Friday night we were making toaster waffles when she came down.

"Oh, did we wake you?" Christina asked. "I'm sorry."

"Yeah, and I don't intend to move all day." I brushed my lips against his cheek, barely touching the heavy makeup. "Break a leg, why don't you?"

"See you during intermission," he said.

I'd taken my seat in the pit and was wetting my clarinet reed when the rest of the orchestra straggled in. We tuned quickly before Mr. Dorsey appeared at the podium. Then the lights went down and only our music stand lights flickered in the darkness. The overture flowed around me as Mr. Dorsey's baton whipped a steady rhythm in the air above my head.

I didn't look up at the stage until Jill's number started. "'Another op'nin', another show,'" she sang, while the dancers spun around her. "'In Philly, Boston, or Baltimo'e.'" She was giving it everything she had, her face already bright with perspiration, her body controlled like it was when she skied or played volleyball.

I loved seeing her concentrate like that, all her energy moving in one direction as if there were a clear line between her and what she wanted.

Poised on the edge of the stage for a moment, she seemed to be looking down into the orchestra. I knew she couldn't see anything beyond the glare of the stage lights, but for a second, I thought we were looking at each other. Tomorrow I'm going to fix everything between us, I said silently, no matter what it takes.

When the stage went dark, Jill was beaming out at the audience, her arms open as she balanced on the shoulders of two of the dancers. Blackout.

After the final curtain and striking the set, we all headed for the cafeteria, which had been decorated for the cast party with flags and streamers intended to form the outline of a medieval jousting tent.

"Wrong historical period," Phoebe said, "but nice."

The deejay was already making music from his platform in the corner.

"Well, the music's in the right decade," Peter said.

"I'm just glad our folks took it over," Jill said.

"Yeah, even though it means my mom's here." Dan grabbed her hand. "Take me to the punch bowl, woman. I'm too dry to dance."

"I'll get Mom to turn the lights down," Jill said. "Does everybody see that spot over there?" She pointed toward the darkest corner in the room. "That's ours."

"If those two did half they talk about doing,

they'd be extremely busy," I said, watching them make a stop at the refreshment table.

"Don't look now, but here come Christina and Randy," Peter said. "You want to dance?"

"Aren't you too tired?"

"To dance with you? Never." Peter pulled me out onto the floor. We were the first couple dancing, but just then the lights dimmed, and within minutes the open space was crowded.

"And here come Greg and Amanda," Peter said, looking over my shoulder.

"Good. He swore he wasn't coming. He claims he has to save his strength for the basketball tournament next week."

Someone bumped against my shoulder.

"Sorry," Christina said. She and Randy swayed beside us. "I see Amanda got Greg to come. I told her if she handled it right, he would."

I pulled Peter in another direction. "Hey, what's going on?" he asked, getting me back in his arms. "I'm supposed to be leading."

"Yeah, well. I just don't want to deal with that." I sighed against his chest. "Christina wanted Greg to come, Peter. I think that's why she's been so chummy with Amanda. Everything else failed."

"Well, I don't suppose his being in the same

room with her will hurt him any," Peter said. "Now, how about we concentrate on each other for a change?"

"I'd love to."

When we finally stopped at the refreshment table, Mom and Jill's mother were there.

"We were just enjoying watching you two dance," Ms. Tatum said with a smile. "I wonder where Jill's gotten to, though."

Peter took the cup of punch she offered him. "She and Dan were out there just now," he said.

"Well, good. Now that she has her driver's license, I can't seem to keep track of her. Jeff insisted she have that car for her birthday when I thought she could drive my old one just as well. Now she can't seem to stand to see it sitting in the driveway a minute." Ms. Tatum handed me a cup. "Just look at Christina. She seems to be having a good time."

"She surely is," Mom said. "She's in another world."

We turned to watch Christina, who had moved so far away from Randy she seemed to be dancing alone, oblivious of the gyrating bodies around her. Her eyes were closed and her face flushed.

"Why, she's quite a pretty girl, isn't she?" Ms. Tatum said. "I'm sorry her mother couldn't stay.

When she stopped by with the potato chips, she said she'd have to take her parents on home."

"I'm not surprised." I expected Mom to give me one of her exasperated looks, but I didn't give her a chance. "I think we're leaving now, Mom. We're both tired. Thanks for the party."

"Yeah, thanks," Peter said.

Mom hugged him. "It was a terrific show. Both of you. I'll see you at home, Annie." She glanced at her watch. "It's almost time to call a halt to this anyway."

⁊◆

I was the first one home, so I let Clancy and Emma out for a few minutes, then left the front door unlocked and the porch light on, and went to bed. Randy would be bringing Christina home soon.

The weariness of the busy week must have finally caught me, because I slept hard. I awoke once, feeling Emma's furry warmth through the blanket. Martha was spending the night with a friend so Emma had searched out a new bedfellow, but I didn't mind. There was something comforting about her weight against my back. The hall light was on and I sensed in a fleeting moment of wakefulness that Mom and Dad were there. All was well.

When I awoke again, the phone was ringing. I

searched for the receiver in the dark, then realized it was Mom and Dad's line. I dozed for a moment, then awoke, startled by a rap on my door and Dad's voice in the hall.

"Annie!" The door opened. "Annie, wake up."

"I'm awake." I struggled to sit up and reach for the lamp. Christina's white bedspread glared in the sudden light. "What is it?"

"That was Greg, honey," Dad said. "He called from the hospital. There's been an accident."

"Greg? Is he all right?" I tried to shake off sleep. Christina's bed was empty.

"It's not him, honey. It's Jill. She hit a tree out on Fairbanks Road." Dad had me by my shoulders. "Your mother and I are going to the hospital. You can come or you can stay here and we'll call you."

"I'll come. I'll be dressed in a minute."

"Well, hurry. Greg doesn't know how serious it is, but he's pretty upset."

❧

The emergency-room entrance to the hospital was starkly lit. Greg and Amanda, who waited together near the door, looked drained of color, their winter faces blanched with fear.

"Are you all right, son?" Dad hugged Greg to him.

"Yeah." Greg's voice was muffled in Dad's shoulder.

"What happened, Amanda?" Mom asked, taking her hands. "Are you all right?" Amanda had seemed calm, but when Mom touched her, she began trembling. Mom led her to one of the vinyl sofas that formed a square in the middle of the dreary room.

"After the party, we went out to that place by the river, you know, out at the end of Fairbanks Road," Amanda began, but she was shaking. She looked helplessly at Greg.

"We weren't out there long, thirty minutes I guess, when Jill shows up in her birthday present— she got a Honda Prelude for her birthday," he said to Dad. "And Christina's with her."

"Christina!" Mom cried. "Oh my Lord, where was she supposed to be? Annie, was she spending the night with us?"

I nodded. "She said she couldn't stay for the party unless she slept over. She said her grandparents got upset if she came in late."

"The question is, where is she now and is she all right?" Dad said.

"They took her back there in a wheelchair, but she could walk and everything. It's Jill," Amanda said, quaking with tears. "She was unconscious, Ms. Gerhardt, and there was blood all over her face. We couldn't even see where it was coming from."

"Where are her folks?" Mom asked.

"Dr. Tatum happened to be here. He's got some-body in labor," Greg said. "Ms. Tatum came just before you did, so they're both in there with her. They're doing X-rays and stuff. Dad, I think it's real serious."

"Maybe not," Dad said, hugging him again. "She could be unconscious from just a mild concus-sion, and even minor head injuries bleed a lot. Any-way, they'll know what to do for her."

I dropped beside Mom on the sofa. "We never really made up. I'm just as stubborn as she is." I was shivering under my sweatshirt.

"She'll be all right." Mom was holding both Amanda and me. "You'll see."

"You said she hit a tree, Greg," Dad said. "How did it happen?"

"She was passing me, and it's a narrow road and she just didn't make the curve. Of course, she shouldn't have been there in the first place."

"And Christina was with her?"

"Yeah. We were parked out by the river and they pulled up next to us and were talking and stuff. Then we decided to go home and they left behind us."

"Larry, what about Danice Moore?" Mom

asked. "Shouldn't we call her?"

"I guess we have to, but I wish I could find out what's going on first."

"I don't think we should wait," Mom said. "I'd want to be here if I were her mother, no matter what."

We huddled together on the sofas while Dad made the call. Greg had his arms around Amanda who leaned heavily against him, her eyes wide and dull in the bright light. "I never saw a wreck before," she said suddenly. "It was like an explosion except that we could see it coming. I mean, we knew it was happening but we couldn't stop it. The car just starting turning off the road, like there wasn't even a driver—"

Greg took over. "She must have slammed on the brakes, because she started skidding and turning in the skid. If it hadn't turned like that, they would have hit head-on. As it was, Jill's side of the car got slammed."

Dad was back. "Ms. Moore's coming right away. She had a lot of questions I couldn't answer."

"She's a nurse, you know," Mom said. "Poor woman. You told her Christina walked in here, didn't you?"

"Yes." Dad sat down beside her. "She wanted to know why Christina was with Jill in the first place.

Why wasn't she where she belonged, she asked me."
He shook his head.

"Oh, we're to blame, aren't we?" Mom cried. "I didn't even know the child was supposed to be at my house. I've had so much on my mind, I just didn't think about Christina." She stood up, pushing out of his arms. "I should have checked with her before she left the dance. She left with Randy, didn't she?"

"I don't know," I said wearily. "I left before she did. Maybe she told him she was staying with Jill."

"She'd do that," Greg said. "She'll do most anything."

"What do you mean?" Mom was getting frantic. "For all we know, the child is seriously hurt and you two are out here criticizing her. Larry, I should have found out what was going on."

"Honey, calm down." He walked her over to the windows, and I followed them. The parking lot outside looked bruised under the amber lights. We watched until another car pulled into a space near the entrance.

"Where is she?" Ms. Moore wanted to know, rushing past us to the emergency desk.

"I'm here," Christina said. Her heavy coat hanging across her thin shoulders and the tangles of hair around her pale face gave her a ghostly, tragic look.

"Are you all right?" Mom cried, but Dad held her back so Ms. Moore could reach Christina first.

"I think so." Her mouth was quivering. "Mom, I was so scared! It was horrible. One minute Jill was laughing and yelling out the window at Greg—I told her to slow down but she wouldn't listen—and then we were off the road and the car was spinning and I knew we were going to die. I just knew it." She clung to her mother, avoiding the rest of us.

"Frances!" Mom cried, attention temporarily averted because Jill's mother was coming toward us. She looked too tired to take another step. "Frances, how is she? Do you know anything?"

Ms. Tatum let Mom embrace her. "Jeff says the head injury may be serious. I know she's lucky to be alive but—" She broke off in tears.

"Oh, Frances." Mom seemed to be supporting her full weight.

"What about you? Are you all right?" Ms. Tatum pulled away and looked at Christina. "Ms. Moore, I'm so sorry about this. Jill's had her license only a week and—well, I just can't tell you how sorry I am that Christina was involved."

"Why were you out at the river, anyway?" Greg asked Christina. He still had his arm around Amanda.

"It was Jill's idea." Christina clung to her mother. "I'm sorry, but it's true," she said when she saw we were staring at her. "She wanted to cruise around after Randy and Dan took us home."

"But you were supposed to come to our house," I said.

"I never said that," Christina said.

"Yes, you did."

"Well, Jill wanted me with her. You've been so mean to her, Annie, and she said we ought to go out and have some fun, just the two of us." Color was creeping back into Christina's face.

"Yeah," Greg said, "I can imagine how important going out on Fairbanks Road was to Jill."

"Well, she did want to," Christina said. She huddled under her mother's arm. "Mama, I don't feel good."

"I'm taking you home right now," Ms. Moore said.

"Don't you think you should wait for Dr. Tatum?" Mom asked. "I'm sure he'll have some instructions for you."

"I do know how to observe a patient, Ms. Gerhardt," Ms. Moore said, as if she were talking to a total stranger.

"We're all tired and upset," Mom said gently.

She forced a little smile. "But I think you really should wait to speak to Jeff. Or someone.".

"I want to go home," Christina cried. She and her mother formed a bulky faded mass of defiance in front of us. "Mama, take me home!"

"Well, at least let me drive you," Dad offered.

"I'm perfectly fine," Ms. Moore said firmly.

Since there didn't seem to be any way of stopping her, Mom and I followed them to the door. "Christina, we'll call tomorrow to see how you are," Mom said. Then she laid a comforting hand on Ms. Moore's shoulder. "I wish you'd let Larry drive you. I know you must feel traumatized, first losing your son and now this."

"I don't know what you're talking about." Ms. Moore pushed through the door with Christina clutched to her side. "Christina's my only child."

24

Mom sent us home at three in the morning. "I'll stay with Frances," she insisted. By then Amanda's parents had come to get her, so the rest of us went home in Greg's car. The house felt so empty, I almost suggested we bring Martha home, but it was the middle of the night, so I didn't say anything. It would be stupid to wake up an entire family and get Martha upset when there was nothing anyone could do.

I didn't even say good night to Dad and Greg, just went to my room and closed the door behind me. I don't suppose any of us slept much. I tossed in my bed until just before dawn, when I went downstairs and crawled into Dad's arms on the sofa. He'd just come in from getting the Sunday paper but hadn't opened it yet. I cuddled against his soft warm sweatshirt and listened to the coffee maker sputtering and hissing in the kitchen.

"Mom's home." His chin was bristly against my forehead. "She wants us all to go to church."

"I'm too tired, Daddy," I groaned.

"Well, you'd better go stand in the shower for thirty minutes because there's no talking her out of it." He tried to stir under me but I wouldn't budge.

"What did she say about Jill?"

"You'd better ask her yourself, honey."

Mom appeared in the archway. She was still wearing the sweats she'd thrown on the night before, and she looked frazzled. "The coffee's ready. I stopped and picked up some bagels if you want one." She sat down on the arm of the sofa at our heads and I felt her hand against my hair. "Annie, Jill woke up a little while ago."

"That's great!"

"Yes, but there's still a lot going on," Mom said. "She's conscious, but she's got a concussion, a broken leg, and a fractured collarbone. They're getting more X-rays today."

I sat up. "What for?"

"Just to make sure they aren't missing anything. Internal bleeding. Things like that. I'm sure Jeff's just being cautious."

"I would be," Dad said. "Let's eat something. A warm bagel with cream cheese will do us good."

"I want us to go to church," Mom said. "We've got time to get to the nine o'clock service."

"I want to see Jill," I said. How could they be talking about eating bagels and going to church when Jill was in the hospital?

"Later," Dad said. "She's probably sleeping, or else they're doing the X-rays this morning. After lunch is soon enough. "

When my tears came, they were hot and rushing. "This is all my fault," I sobbed.

"No, it isn't." Dad put his arm around me.

"Yes, it is. Things have happened—things with Christina that I should have told you about."

"Greg told me about the sleepwalking episode last night," Dad said. "Of course, I've known for some time he didn't like her."

I shivered against his chest. "There's other stuff, too."

"Then I guess you'd better tell us," Mom said. "The bagels can wait."

❧

That afternoon, I waited on a bench in the hospital corridor hoping for a chance to see Jill. Dr. Tatum had promised I could.

"I'm sure she'll need a diversion," he'd said when I reached him on the phone. "She's in traction, so she's not resting very well."

I stared at the cover of an old *Cosmopolitan*, unable to open it. Who cared about dating and clothes and movie stars?

"Hey there." It was Peter. "I phoned your house and your mom told me you were here. Why didn't you call me, Annie?"

"I don't know." I hugged him hard. "I guess I thought this was something I had to do myself. Apologize to Jill, I mean."

"So you caused the wreck, huh?"

"I should have made sure Christina came home with me. I know she's the reason Jill was out on Fairbanks Road."

"You're not her keeper, Annie, no matter what you think."

Ms. Tatum appeared in the hall looking exhausted, but she managed a weak smile. "Hello, Annie. Peter. You can come in now if you'd like."

I was glad Peter was with me. I could feel him at my back while we maneuvered around the traction apparatus that held Jill's leg in place. She looked pale, and there was a bandage covering the side of her head above a thick purple bruise that had spread down her temple onto her cheek. I knew there were stitches under there, too.

"Hi," I said. "How're you doing?"

"Okay." She grimaced as if her jaw hurt when she talked. "You don't have to whisper, you know. Or is this a hearing test?"

I felt tears but I was smiling. She was still funny. I pressed her hand under mine. "Your dad says you're going to be fine."

"Yeah. My car's totaled, though."

"But at least you're in one piece," Peter said.

"Actually, I'm in two pieces at the moment. They're not setting this leg until tomorrow." She squeezed my hand. "Greg told you what happened?"

"Yes. We were downstairs in the waiting room most of the night."

"Then you know Christina's okay." Jill let go of my hand, and I leaned back against Peter, feeling his hands on my shoulders.

"She's fine. Listen, Jill, I'm really sorry about everything." I tried to control the choking in my voice. "I've been so miserable."

"Me, too. Even before this mess." She looked as if she were struggling against tears just like I was.

"You're the best," I said.

"Yeah. Best what?"

"Friend. My best friend."

"Look who's here," Ms. Tatum said from the doorway. She moved aside to let Christina pass. "Jeff says five minutes, gang. Jill's just had her pain medication, so she should be dozing off soon."

"I think I'll wait in the hall," Peter said. I knew what he was doing, but for a moment, I wanted to hold on to him.

Christina walked carefully to the opposite side of the bed. She was holding her shoulders stiff, and there was a skinned place on her forehead. "I'm sore all over," she said, "but I guess you are, too."

"Yeah." Jill was looking at me instead of Christina.

"I wanted to make sure you're all right," Christina said. "Mama said I should just call, but I wanted to see for myself."

"I'm going to be fine," Jill said with a brightness I knew she was faking. "No tennis this spring, but Dad says I should be ready for volleyball in the fall." She gave us a little smile. I could see she was determined not to cry in front of Christina.

"Jill's our best volleyball player," I said. "Our team was in the regional finals last year."

"And we're going to win it next time."

"I'm probably transferring to Lawrence High

next week." Christina shrugged. "Mama says I should. It's a better school, anyway. Of course, Daddy said I could go anywhere I want to. He said just pick a boarding school anywhere in the country and he'd send me."

I looked at Jill, trying to read what she was thinking, but she just looked tired and hurt. That's when I knew I couldn't let this go on.

"You haven't seen your dad in years," I blurted out. "Your mom said so."

"Yes, I have. He calls me, too." Christina's cheeks flushed but she didn't waver. "Mama doesn't know."

"And your brother. Tell us about him."

"He died. I told you." She looked feverish.

"But it isn't true, is it, Christina? You never had a brother at all."

"I did too. Mama had a miscarriage and it was a little boy. I did have a brother." She shook her head back, and those bright cheeks and that dark hair tumbling around her shoulders made her look so fragile, so innocent, that I almost shuddered. "This is how it always is—people act like they're your friend and then they treat you like this. They attack you," she said tearfully.

"We were never friends," I said, surprised at how calm I was. "Friends don't lie to each other.

They don't use each other."

"Annie." Jill grimaced as she put out her hand to grab mine. "Let it go."

"Mama's waiting for me," Christina said to Jill. "I'm glad you're all right." Then she disappeared, leaving the door open behind her.

Peter was standing in the doorway, so I knew he'd heard. "She's never backing down. Don't you see that?" he said, coming in. "If she backs down, her whole world will cave in."

"I guess." I felt really tired, but I squeezed Jill's hand gently. "Are you okay? Honestly?"

"I'm going to be." She was beginning to look groggy, and I could feel her hand falling away from mine. "Tomorrow I expect to hear all the gory details, but right now let me make the best of this legal substance they're feeding me."

"Okay. See you tomorrow."

"I'll be here."

❧

Just before dark, the doorbell rang, and I opened it to find Christina standing on the porch. Her mother's car was waiting in the driveway, the motor whining in the cold.

"I came to get my things," she said when I'd let her in.

"I'll help you." I followed her upstairs and sat on the bed while she collected her clothes from my closet and stuffed them in her overnight bag.

"Don't forget the makeup," I said when the bag was full.

"I'll leave it for Martha," she said.

"No, I want you to take it." I brought the box to her. "What did you want from us, Christina?"

"Nothing." She pressed the makeup box to her chest and lifted her bag, her shoulders bowed with effort. I didn't offer to help her.

"Then what did you want from me? At least tell the truth about that."

She started for the door, then turned back. "You think you have everything, Annie. Well, you don't. You don't have guts." She swayed a little under the weight of the bag. "You think I want to be like you? Just look at all this. You didn't do anything to get it—it was all here, it was all handed to you. You don't know how to make things happen. You couldn't even hold on to your best friend. Frankly, you're the last person I'd want to be."

I heard her on the stairs and then the front door slammed. But the sound of her voice was still there, strident and full of pain. Maybe for once she'd told the truth.

That night I'd just hung up from talking to Peter when the phone rang. It was Jill.

"I just wanted to say good night," she said.

"Do you still hurt?"

"A little, but it's okay. Hey, Dad says maybe I can be back in school in a couple of weeks."

"Until then, I'll bring you your homework assignments."

"Jeez. I should have known you'd offer to do something like that." There was her old sarcasm.

"What are friends for?" I asked her.

"Yeah, right." She sounded sleepy. "Night, Annie."

"Night, Jill."

When we'd hung up, I lay in bed listening to the house creak and groan around me. Outside, a gusty wind was whistling. Branches rattled against the roof. I could hear Martha's radio playing softly in the next room. Clancy padded up the stairs and pushed against Greg's door, finding a bed for the night. Mom and Dad had already closed their door.

I turned over and wrestled the blanket around my shoulder. I was tired, but my heart was racing, my mind spinning back through the weekend. I thought of Peter. Maybe this really would be the

274

year he let Rosie go. Maybe we'd watch her, suddenly free of jesses and bell, rising to a thermal and hanging there a moment before lifting away in search of a mate, a life of her own full of risks and adventure and spirals in the sky.

"Well you see, she's always been wild," Peter would say as she disappeared. And he would let her go in his heart, too.

I sighed, feeling the knot in my chest release a little.

"Good-bye, Christina," I said in the dark. It didn't matter that no one else could hear.

25

I got a ride to school with Greg just in time for the homeroom bell. Everybody had heard about the accident and wanted to know about Jill. Christina's desk was empty, too, but nobody asked about her. I went through the motions of changing classes and pretending to be attentive although I felt drugged and hardly did more than take down my homework assignments.

Randy was waiting for me outside English class. "I heard about the wreck. Is Christina hurt?" he asked.

"She's got a few bruises. That's all." I took his arm to lead him out of the steadily moving caravan in the hall. "I thought she'd call you."

"Yeah, well. Who knows with Christina?" We leaned against the wall. "I took her to Jill's Saturday night. She said she was spending the night there. I guess the two of them went out again." Randy hung his head, then gave me an embarrassed grin. "I like her okay, Annie, but I don't think it's going to amount to anything. She's hard to figure."

"You're right about that."

"She's pretty, though. You may not see it at first, but it's there. She can get to you."

At lunch, I met Peter in the cafeteria.

"Rough morning?" he asked.

"I look that bad?" I stepped in line in front of him. The smells of old grease and disinfectant were already making me queasy.

"Just tired." He wrapped his arm across my chest so my back rested against him. "Is Christina here?"

"No." I didn't want to move, although the line in front of me had traveled a couple of feet. "I don't think we'll ever see her again."

"Don't count on it," Peter said, nudging me forward.

He was right. Later that week at the basketball tournament in the university gym, I saw Christina in the opposite stands. I guess I noticed the blue sweater first. At a distance, she looked thin and plain, but I knew she wasn't. There was a girl with her.

Every afternoon after school I went to see Jill. She said I didn't have to come every day, but with the play over, I didn't have that much to do. We'd do our homework together, so for more than a week I had my evenings free. At first it felt strange to be in my room alone in the evenings. I'd gotten used to Christina, her energy in the house, the competitive edge she put on everything.

Then Jill was back in school, hobbling along on crutches with Dan carrying her book bag and elbowing a path in the crowded hallway for her between classes. She loved it.

Practice for the spring choral concert began. I sang alto, and during rehearsals I tried to pick out Peter's voice in the baritone section, but I couldn't. We were singing a medley of Andrew Lloyd Webber songs, and no matter how many times I heard him practice the solo part of "The Music of the Night," I felt giddy and warm. Rosie was still molting, and so during the last cold dreary days of March, we'd take a supply of snacks to his room and listen to tapes and talk.

We had lots to talk about. We were both already thinking about colleges, but it wasn't just the future we had between us. There was our past, too. Sometimes we were just quiet together, lying on his bed until the room was almost dark and we could barely see each other, but I knew he was there.

੨ৣ

In early April, we went to the Tatums' condominium at Pine Knoll Shores for the weekend just as Ms. Tatum had promised—Dan, Phoebe, Eric, Peter, and me. Jill was still in a cast, so we didn't go down to the beach. There was a hot tub on the deck beside the swimming pool, and we hung out there, up to our chins in the warm steamy water while Jill sat bundled in a lounge chair in the cool spring air. She didn't seem to mind.

The first night we ordered pizza and rented *Lady and the Tramp*. We knew all the songs and sang them over and over, each of us playing different parts each time. The best was Jill and me doing the Siamese song even though we couldn't do the dance we'd created years ago. Then we tried to watch a horror film the boys had picked, but we girls went to bed before the scariest part.

The next night we boiled shrimp and ate until we were stuffed, butter and spicy sauce dripping off our fingers and chins onto the the bibs Ms. Tatum insisted we wear. Then we found a box of poker chips and played blackjack, nibbling at the remains of Jill's chocolate birthday cake that had collapsed on its plate, and drinking Mountain Dew for the caffeine surge that would keep us awake all night.

Just before dawn, Jill motioned for me to help her up from her place on the floor. I thought she wanted to go to the bathroom, but in the hall, she whispered, "Let's go outside."

The tide had just gone out, and the sand was damp enough for her crutches to hold in it. She struggled along for a minute, then plopped down on the sand. I sat next to her. The sun was behind us, and the new light above the water line was gray and heavy.

"The last time I was here, you didn't come," she said. "I walked miles that Saturday, all the way to Indian Beach and back."

"That was when we'd first met Christina," I said.

"Yeah." Jill pulled up her good knee and wrapped her arms around it. She was looking out at the water, but there was a little smile playing at the corner of her mouth.

"You were right about her," I said. The waves seemed slow and distant. "I guess you were right about a lot of things."

"Hardly." She sighed. "The weird thing is—we

still don't know who she was."

"I can't worry about that," I said. "I've got enough to do figuring out who I am."

"Yeah, well. Don't wear yourself out with it. I hear it's a lifetime job." Jill tugged at my sleeve. "Hey, let's go wading."

"You can't!"

"Oh come on, Annie. Where's your spunk?" She planted her crutches in the sand and pulled up on them. I could see there was no stopping her.

At the edge of the surf, she dropped one crutch and took my hand. The water swirled around our feet, bubbled up toward the cast she held just above the foam. Just then I looked back to see the sun shoot straight up behind us, a spreading glow that enveloped us with morning light and dappled the water beyond the breakers. A wave rolled in, bursting with spindrift and tugging the sand beneath us, but we held on. She was light in my arms.